A Fenland Secret

By

Nico Dobben

About the author

Norfolk, and in particular, West Norfolk, has been the home of Nico Dobben after moving from the Netherlands in 1981. Since then he has worked in a variety of jobs including delivery driver, roadie, factory worker and teacher. His creative output has focussed mainly on song writing and performing. He has released two albums of original songs.

'A Fenland Secret' is his second novel.

Also by Nico Dobben

Novels:

A Fenland Murder (2021)

Recordings:

Slow You Down (2020)
Songs of Love, Misery and Pain (2011)

Acknowledgements

I would like to thank Ann, Bill, Helen, Jonathan, Marie, Ruth and Terry for their valuable comments and suggestions.

I am indebted, once again, to Abigail Frusher for allowing me to use one of her original Fenscape watercolours as part of the cover design.

I am appreciative of all the bookshops in the area that have stocked and promoted my first novel.

Finally, I am grateful to Linda Elder for proofreading the completed script. It goes without saying that any remaining errors are entirely mine.

All characters in this novel are fictitious and any resemblance to real persons, living or dead, is purely coincidental.

Copyright Nico Dobben 2022

The right of Nico Dobben to be identified as the author of the work has been asserted to him in accordance with the Copyright, Designs and Patents Act 1988.

All rights reserved

Front cover painting: Abigail Frusher

ISBN 978-1-915787-30-9

Printed by Biddles Book Printers
www.biddles.co.uk
Blackborough End, Kings Lynn, Norfolk

Dedicated to Harry (Cuby) Muskee (1943 - 2012)

Prologue

1996

The plan was to frighten him a bit. Warn him, so he would pick up his sleeping bag and disappear back to whichever squat in London he had sprung from. But things had gotten out of hand. At first they had a reasonable conversation but when the man realised he was no longer welcome he had started arguing and making threatening comments so there really was no other choice. How could anyone have known that a few blows to the head would kill someone instantly?

Anyway, *'what's done is done.'* Now what to do with the body? Leaving it here is no option. The last train has left and Downham Market Railway Station is deserted so there are no witnesses. Putting the body in the back of the car is hard work but not as difficult as first thought. Driving the twenty-five miles or so to the old airbase near Ely takes no time at all. Several protesters are sitting around a large bonfire not far from the perimeter fence. Nobody takes any notice of the small hatchback slowly making its way towards an entrance gate near the old control tower.

Recently the excavators have been busy digging inspection trenches so the scientists can examine the soil structure. But the driver knows they have finished their investigation so it's an ideal place to hide the body.

Maybe it will be found before it gets covered with earth but so what? Nobody knows there was a connection between them so no one will find out. Leaving him here at the airfield is a clever move. If he is ever found everyone will think it was one of the protesters who was responsible.

'Bloody waste of space, that lot.'

Chapter 1

2021

'It's not often us politicians are able to use the words, *it's a win-win situation* but on this occasion I think the expression is justified.'

The speaker, a dark haired man in his thirties. signalled to his assistant.

'First slide please.'

Behind him, on a screen nearly large enough to fill the whole stage of Downham Market Town Hall, a map appeared.

'As you can see,' the man pointed to a red circle in the middle, 'the proposed New Town is an equal distance from Ely, Wisbech and Downham Market. These will therefore be the principal towns to benefit from the planned three thousand new homes.'

'In what way will we benefit?' someone shouted.

'The development will create jobs for local people while the houses are being built and when completed the influx of new families will benefit the local economy for a long time to come.'

'What about doctors and dentists and schools?' someone else asked.

'The plans include two primary schools, a doctor's surgery and health centre as well as a newsagents and a small supermarket, all provided by the developer.'

'Won't there be a lot more traffic?'

'Absolutely, good point,' came the reply. 'But here again the developers have come up trumps. They have agreed to foot the bill for widening the existing roads to make space for bus and cycle lanes!'

'What's going to happen to the golf course?'

'The golf course will stay exactly where it is now. As a matter of fact it will be extended with new additions offering recreational space for families to enjoy.'

A new slide appeared on the screen showing an image of happy children feeding ducks against a background of beautifully designed lakes and parkland.

The presentation continued for another ten minutes or so after which the speaker thanked everyone for coming and invited them to have a look at the displays.

'Feel free to ask our partners from Future Build any questions,' he finished, pointing to a team of smart looking representatives all wearing similar looking suits and name badges.

'And don't forget to leave your name and contact details at the entrance if you wish to be kept informed.'

There was a ripple of applause before the majority of people made their way to the middle of the hall where a large model display formed the centrepiece of the exhibition.

While most people were still in the hall discussing the plans, Councillor Anthony Fisher got in his Mercedes and set off towards home. *That couldn't have gone any better,* he congratulated himself. Just then his phone rang.

'How did it go?' the voice at the other end asked.

'No worries,' replied Councillor Fisher. 'Same as in Wisbech and Ely. We even got a round of applause.'

'No sign of any objections? No trouble makers?'

'Nothing,' replied the councillor. 'I noticed two of the Green Party councillors were present and had a quick word with them. Even they are broadly in favour, especially after I showed them the plans for some of the energy saving features you're planning to include as standard.'

'Good work,' and then after a slight pause the caller added, 'we must be vigilant though. You and I might agree that this is a much needed development and we at Future Build will do what we can, but it's your job to make sure we jump all the hurdles.'

And with that he rang off. The final reminder that they were only at the beginning of a long process did not dent Anthony Fisher's good mood. If the left wing loonies and tree huggers were on board what could go wrong?

Detective Chief Inspector Steve Culverhouse was driving from his home in Downham Market towards the small town of Littleport. He stopped at the local Coop store to stock up on some essentials, wine for dinner and a bottle of Irish whiskey for bedtime, before continuing on his way to his father's farm. About twenty minutes after turning off the Ely by-pass he could see the control tower of the old airfield in the distance. Another fifteen minutes he told himself.

Before long he was driving along the old perimeter fence but then had to reduce his speed near the entrance to the golf course because a small crowd of people were slowing down the traffic while holding up placards. *"SAVE OUR GREENBELT"* read one, while another suggested *"NO NEW TOWN DEVELOPMENT."* Steve opened his car window and accepted a leaflet from one of the protesters.

'Are you local sir?' an elderly man asked Steve.

'Sort of,' he replied, 'my dad lives up the road.' The man produced another leaflet.

'Please ask him to read this. And tell him to get in touch if he's interested.'

'Will do,' Steve promised and with that the man stepped out of the way so he could continue. *I've seen that face before,* thought Steve but however hard he tried he could not place him.

Just when Anthony Fisher turned into his drive his mobile phone rang. He looked at the screen. It was Bob Bradley, CEO of Future Build.

'Hello again,' he answered, 'what's up?'

'You tell me what's up,' came the reply. 'You assured me less than an hour ago that everything was going smoothly. So how do you explain what's happening at the golf course?'

'What is happening at the golf course?'

'That's what I just asked. Protesters, harassing the public, handing out leaflets trying to stop the development.'

'But who are they?'

'No idea, but we'd better find out and put a stop to

it pronto. I'll meet you there in forty minutes.'

Councillor Fisher sighed. *That's his plans for tonight gone up in smoke.* He turned his car around and headed in the direction of the golf club. By the time he got to the gate there was no sign of any protesters. Just a couple of placards left behind and a few leaflets pinned to a tree. He got out of his car but before he had time to read what they said he heard the distinct sound of Bob Bradley's classic Lotus Elite. Together they made their way to the clubhouse and settled for a table in a quiet corner. The club steward came over with some drinks and took a chair himself.

'Thanks for warning me,' Bob Bradley addressed him directly. 'Tell us what happened.'

'Not much really,' the steward replied. 'There were about thirty of them. They turned up in three minibuses from a rental firm in Peterborough. They just stood in the road and handed out these leaflets to drivers. I went over and asked them what they were doing. They were very polite and told me they wanted to stop any further development of the green belt.'

'Green belt my arse,' Bradley interjected. 'It's an old airfield for God's sake, a brownfield site if ever there was one.'

'I actually pointed that out,' the steward agreed,

'but they told me that it's not so much the airfield but the loss of hundreds of acres of farmland that worried them. Anyway, like I said, they weren't really causing any problems and left after about half an hour.'

'Any press?' Anthony Fisher asked.

'Not that I noticed, but one of them was filming on his mobile phone. Anyway, I thought it best to tell you as soon as possible.'

'You did well,' Bob Bradley replied, sliding a twenty pound note across the table. 'Good work and let us know if anything else happens.'

With that the steward got up and for a few moments the two men remained quiet. Councillor Fisher was the first to speak.

'But who are they?' By now he's scanned the leaflet. 'It just gives an email address and a Facebook page. No names, no organisation.'

'That's odd,' Bob Bradley said, 'normally groups like *Greenpeace* and *Extinction Rebellion* plaster their names all over the place. The more publicity the better.'

'What do you suggest we do next?'

'I'm not going to do anything,' Bob Bradley replied. 'I am the respectable face of a successful sustainable development company. But you, my friend, are going to spend the weekend doing some digging.'

Chapter 2

By the time Steve arrived at his father's farm he'd already forgotten the encounter with the protesters. They had their dinner at the kitchen table. Steve looked around, not much had changed since he left for London just over twenty-five years ago.

'How are the boys?' his father asked.

'They are well and send their love,' he replied. 'I saw them two weeks ago and told them about my plans with your old bike. They sounded excited and want to come up and have a go riding it along the track.'

'They're very welcome,' his father said. 'Shame it didn't work out between you and Julia. But at least you see the boys regularly and soon they'll be old enough to come up on the train on their own.'

'They do already,' Steve explained. 'Julia puts them on the train at Kings Cross and it's a straight journey to Downham Market.'

He looked at his father. Did his dad still regret that his own marriage to Steve's mum ended within a year of him leaving home? His father seemed to read his mind.

'Have you heard from your mother at all?'

'Not since the last time I told you about at Christmas. You know what she's like, not very good at communicating. I suppose no news is good news.' He steered the conversation away from both their failed marriages.

'What do you think about my plans for the bike?'

'If you want to restore it feel free. It's a lot of work but it will be nice to see a bit more of you, especially as I'd like to discuss some of the changes happening around here. Let's put the kettle on and move to the living room.'

When Anthony Fisher turned into his drive he noticed his wife's Audi TT was already put away in the garage. She must have got home early from the legal firm she worked for in Cambridge. The moment he walked through the door he smelled the unmistakable aroma of his favourite curry. He suddenly realised how hungry he actually was.

'There you are,' Saskia greeted him. 'I stopped at the Indian in Ely. I hope you don't mind.'
She produced two glasses of red wine and handed him one.

'I thought we could make an evening of it, after all it's Friday night. Another week gone, we deserve it. Come and sit on the terrace.'

He followed her out through the large patio doors. It was a beautiful evening with the sun still holding its own even though it was now nearly eight o'clock. The flat Fenland landscape stretched out before them. Looking to the right he could see the tall silos of the Wissington sugar beet factory, while to the left you could just recognise the majestic outline of the "Ship of the Fens", Ely Cathedral.

Anthony took a sip of his wine. It was on evenings like this that he realised how lucky he was, a beautiful house, an even more beautiful and successful wife and soon more money than he could ever have dreamt of. But then he remembered his task for the weekend and felt annoyed. Saskia noticed the change in his face.

'What's wrong?' she asked. He briefly explained the problem.

'Come on Ant,' she said cheerfully, 'let's forget about that for tonight.' She stroked his hair.

'I tell you what, I'll give you a hand tomorrow. I have quite a few contacts in Peterborough and I'm sure we'll find out who these trouble makers are in no time.'

Anthony perked up. They heard the ping from the

oven and by the time the food was on the table he had already forgotten why he was so annoyed in the first place.

The next morning, after breakfast, Steve put on his overalls, collected his tools from the car and sat down with a cup of coffee looking through the Haynes manual for a 1956 BSA.

The bike itself stood before him, covered in dust and bits of straw. His father told him that the last time he had ridden it was over forty years ago.

'Why did you stop?' Steve had asked.

'Your mother lost interest,' his dad had explained.

'I didn't want to go out by myself and anyway, you and your sister had come along by then and we already had a car so that just seemed easier.'

'But you never sold it?'

'No, I always thought that one day I might give it a try again. Maybe, once you've done it up I'll have a go.'

They had continued talking for a while until Steve reminded his dad that he wanted to discuss something specific.

'You mentioned changes?'

'Yes,' his dad had replied, 'you might as well know. I'm thinking of giving up the farm.'

'But …' Steve began but his dad stopped him.

'Hear me out, I've been thinking about it for a while and now with the new development at the airfield this seems to be the right time to make the decision.'

'What does the new town have to do with it?' Steve had asked.

'Everything,' his dad replied. 'You know I rent most of my land but I did buy ten acres several years ago at the edge of the airfield for £7000 an acre. They've made me a provisional offer which is about ten times more than I paid for it.'

'Bloody hell Dad,' Steve did a quick calculation.

'That's nearly three quarters of a million. You're going to be rich!'

Was it the right decision? Steve asked himself while starting to dismantle the bike. Probably, after all, his dad wasn't getting any younger and was already receiving his pension. Yes, why shouldn't he? This seemed too good an opportunity to miss.

While Steve was working on the bike, Anthony Fisher and his wife were sitting side by side at the large kitchen table. Each had a laptop in front of them. Saskia had sent an email to the address on the leaflet asking for more information.

'I've made up a name and have opened a new email account,' she told her husband. 'Best not to get my own name out there at this point.'

'Good thinking,' he replied while checking out the Facebook page.

'Ah, here we are.'

He turned the screen towards Saskia. The Facebook page explained that *"The Anti New Town Collective"* had been set up to oppose any development that led to the destruction of natural habitat in the Fenland area. It helpfully explained that its members were drawn from a range of organisations such as Friends of the Earth and Greenpeace but that they had consciously chosen to start a new group so anyone who agreed with their campaign could join, regardless of which political party they supported. There were some photographs taken at yesterday's demonstration outside the golf course. Some of the faces in the pictures were tagged and before long Saskia and Anthony had an idea of who appeared to be five of the more prominent members. As their Facebook pages were set to "public" Saskia suggested they carefully read the profiles and look out for any links with other groups. Anthony got up to make some more coffee. He was actually rather enjoying himself. He loved working with his wife like this. He admired the way she approached each task in a logical and methodical way, no doubt the result of her legal training.

By lunchtime Saskia declared:

'I think we're done. Let's see what we've got.'

She showed Anthony how she had organised the basic information on each of the individuals. Apart from name, age and contact details she had also drawn lines where two or more shared the same preferences.

'Look here,' she explained, 'these two guys are obviously friends. They're the same age and both have season tickets for "POSH", better known as Peterborough United. But I've also got some pictures of these two together with the other three on an Anti-War demo in Hyde Park. I think that was a few years ago so they must have known each other for quite some time. But you know what I find very strange? When I compared their contacts, two of them listed Arthur Turner as a Facebook friend. Isn't he one of your politician friends?'

'Well I never,' exclaimed Anthony. 'I wouldn't call him a friend, but yes, I know him. He's the guy I told you about before, to the right of Genghis Khan; thinks all foreigners should be deported and lights a candle every night beneath a picture of Margaret Thatcher.' Saskia laughed.

'Is that true?'

'I don't know but it wouldn't surprise me.'

'Strange isn't it?' she repeated.

'It's weird,' Anthony agreed. 'Why would he be friends with the sort of people he absolutely abhors? But,' he continued, 'I find it equally strange that he has a Facebook account in the first place. Whenever I've been at meetings he always looks disapprovingly when I take out my phone to check a date or record an appointment. He still carries a leather diary with him wherever he goes. Thank you so much Saskia. You've saved the weekend.'

And with that he got up to ring Bob Bradley and tell him what he'd found out.

Chapter 3

When Steve walked into Downham Market Police Station on Monday morning he was greeted by Maddie, the civilian receptionist, who told him that Detective Chief Superintendent Sarah Sutton was waiting for him upstairs in her office. Great, Steve thought, already looking forward to a cup of her famous coffee. And he was not disappointed as the moment he walked in he smelled the aroma of authentic Columbian coffee beans.

'I'll come straight to the point,' she said, handing him a cup. 'We have a staffing issue. As you know DI Starling has been given compassionate leave to look after her mother who is seriously ill. And now I've been informed that Detective Inspector Baker has been asked to take up a new role at Lincolnshire Police Headquarters, reorganising their office and response procedures.'

'That doesn't surprise me,' Steve replied. 'That's what he's really good at and there isn't much of that sort of work to do here.'

'I agree but I'll be sorry to see him go. He was with us from the beginning.'

Steve nodded. The Special Fenland Police Force might only have been going for a few years but in that time Sarah, Steve and the rest of the team had formed a real bond. And that included Sergeant Newman and Maddie.

'What about a replacement?' he asked.

'That's what I need to discuss with you. We have been asked to take on Eva Lappinska as a Detective Constable with the view to mentoring her while she completes her CID studies.'

Now that was a surprise.

'Does Eva know about this?' he asked.

'No, I wanted to talk to you first.'

She turned towards him and looked him straight in the eye.

'Tell me if you think it's none of my business but I know that ever since you more or less saved her life you have seen each other regularly.'

Steve's mind turned back to the last really big case a couple of years ago when two people died and Police Constable Eva Lappinska was kept hostage, only to be freed by DCS Sutton and himself in the nick of time.

'I don't mind you asking at all,' he said. 'Eva and I enjoy a meal out or a walk when our shifts and other commitments allow. As you know I think very highly of her. I know you do too. But Eva and I are friends, nothing more.'

'In that case I shall invite her for an informal visit as soon as possible,' DCS Sutton replied while she poured them both another coffee.

'On a different matter, what's happened to crime in the countryside? What are you working on at the moment?'

'Not much,' Steve replied, 'I agree it's fairly quiet. I was sort of planning to check up on Mick Mendham's activities, see if he's sold any suspicious tractors lately.'

Sarah smiled. Mick Mendham was one of the people involved in the case two years ago. Although he was cleared of any wrong doing on that occasion, some of the evidence suggested that he may well have been involved in the theft of expensive tractors in the area.

'Not a bad idea,' she agreed. 'It might be worth checking if he's stayed on the straight and narrow!'

The next couple of days Steve spent his time catching up on paperwork and sorting out his office. He realised what a luxury this was, especially when he compared it to his busy days in London with the Met.

On Wednesday Eva arrived at the station for her chat with DCS Sutton. He met her afterwards, in the foyer, just before she was about to leave.

'How did it go?'

'So you knew about this?' she replied quite sternly.

'Sorry,' was all Steve could muster. Eva laughed.

'Don't be silly, of course you knew. Actually, I knew you knew already. Only teasing. Anyway, I think I owe you a curry. Are you free tonight?'

The first time Steve and Eva had a meal together was in the midst of a rather nasty case of kidnapping and murder during which Eva nearly lost her life. They'd hit it off in spite of a considerable age difference and ever since then they had met regularly. They both shared a love of cycling and walking in the Norfolk countryside often finishing the day with a meal in a local pub. Tonight they agreed to meet back at the same restaurant where their paths crossed by accident a few years earlier.

'Congratulations,' Steve greeted Eva. He'd waited for her on a bench opposite the town clock. Both had decided to walk. It was another lovely summer's evening and it meant they could enjoy a drink without having to worry about driving.

'Thank you,' she replied. After a quick hug they

walked round the corner and entered the restaurant. The manager welcomed them with a friendly handshake before one of the waiters led them to their table.

'So how did it go with the boss?' Steve asked.

'I thought it went really well,' she replied. 'It must have done I suppose, otherwise she wouldn't have offered me the job.'

'What kind of things did she ask?' Steve enquired.

'Oh you know, where I see myself in ten years' time and that sort of thing.'

'And what did you say?'

'I told her in ten years' time I want to take over your job.' They both laughed.

'Anything else?' he wanted to know.

'We talked about any particular skills I may bring to the post and the things I need to develop more.'

'And?'

'I told her that my language skills have proved to be an asset in the past.'

'I agree,' Steve interjected, 'there are not many police officers who speak Polish, Russian, English, German and French.'

'But I also told her I wanted to learn everything about the job. I think my law degree will be useful when it comes to interviewing suspects and dealing with solicitors, but I need more experience in day-to-day investigative work.'

Steve hesitated.

'Did she say anything about us?'

Was it his imagination or was there the slightest hint of a blush on her face.

'She asked if our friendship might be a problem when working together. I told her that I think we are both professional enough for that not to get in the way. She seemed happy with that. Did she talk to you about it?'

'She did, in fact she asked me the same question and I told her the same thing.'

'Great minds think alike,' Eva replied.

Steve smiled. It was the same thing she said two years ago when they met by chance in the very same restaurant to order a take-away and ended up sharing a meal.

'I think you will be brilliant,' Steve offered, 'we are lucky to have you.'

Chapter 4

The moment Steve walked into the police station the next morning, Maddie called him over and told him he had a visitor. Steve was a little surprised as he rarely got people just dropping in without an appointment.

'Who is it?' he asked.

'Mick Mendham,' was the answer.

As Steve made his way to the waiting room he wondered what Mick wanted. He also remembered that he had been planning to ring him but hadn't yet got around to it. Ah well, depending on why Mick was here he might be able to find out how the tractor business was going. He opened the door and found his visitor leaning back in his chair with his eyes closed. He looked a little dishevelled.

'To what do I owe the pleasure?' Steve asked by way of a greeting. 'You haven't come to get your manual back I hope?'

He was referring to the Haynes BSA Bike Manual Mick had lent him when they last met.

'No worries,' replied Mick. 'You can keep it as long as you want. No, I've come to get some advice.'
Steve was intrigued.

'Come to my office,' he suggested, 'and I'll get us a coffee. You look as if you could do with some caffeine.'

'You can say that again, especially after the night I've just had.'

Once they were seated Mick told him that he had spent the night in his car on the airfield next to the golf course.

'Why?' Steve asked.

'I'm subcontracting for the company behind the planned new town,' Mick explained. 'I've supplied them with three diggers and a couple of nine ton dumper trucks. The guys driving them are all experienced and have been with me for a long time. They've been on site now for nearly a month.'
Steve was surprised.

'I didn't know they had started work already,' he interrupted.

'They haven't. What we are doing is digging soil inspection holes and supporting the company carrying out a survey of the site. Well, the first couple of weeks everything was fine but over the last ten days we've had problems with some of our equipment being damaged.'

'In what way damaged?'

'Small things really. We've had a couple of slashed tyres, a broken windscreen and an attempt to force open the door of one of the diggers. Whoever is behind this has also stolen a couple of tarpaulins we cover the dumper trucks with overnight.'

'Have you reported this to the local police?'

'I have, but they say that they don't have the manpower to patrol the site. They suggested we employ a security guard. I explained there is already someone there but the place is so big that it's impossible to cover the whole area.'

'So why have you come to see me? You know we only have a small team here.'

'I know that, but there is something else. There is a whole load of machinery belonging to other firms on site but our machines seem to be the only ones targeted by the vandals. I mentioned this to the local police but they suggested it was a coincidence.'

'Do you have any idea why?'

'None whatsoever. I first thought it would be the protesters but surely they wouldn't target just one firm?'

'Could it be a competitor?'

'It did go through my mind but I always get on well with the other local firms. As a matter of fact I have subcontracted for the main developer several times over the last ten years and never had so much as a complaint.'

'Are you talking about Future Build?'

'Yes, they also suggested it might be the demonstrators. They pay for the security guard and promised they would tell him to keep a close eye on our machinery as well as theirs. But it hasn't made any difference. That's why I've spent the last couple of nights there myself.'

Both men remain quiet for a while before Steve said,

'I agree it's a bit strange but I can't really see how I can help.'

Mick got up.

'I'm not sure myself. I just thought I'd come and see you because I don't know where to go next.'

'I tell you what,' Steve replied, 'I'm back at my dad's this weekend working on the bike. His farm borders the airfield. I'll ask him if he's seen anything unusual and might just have a drive around myself.'

'Thanks,' Mick replied and made his way back to his car.

On Friday afternoon Steve and DCS Sutton were sharing a coffee discussing the events of the week. They agreed it had been very quiet indeed.

'Do you think all criminals are on holiday?' Steve joked.

Just then the phone rang. DCS Sutton answered and after listening for a short while she replied.

'That's okay Maddie, put her through.'

She switched on the speaker phone.

'You might want to hear this,' she said to Steve.

The person at the other end of the line identified herself as Detective Sergeant Mary Ledbetter from Cambridgeshire CID. She explained that earlier that day they were called to the proposed new town site as a body had been found by one of the digger drivers. As the remains appeared to be quite old they had called for help from a forensic archaeologist who was planning to examine them in detail on Monday.

'Sounds interesting,' DCS Sutton commented, 'but I'm sure you are aware that we don't deal with archaeological remains.'

'I know,' replied DS Ledbetter. 'But I was there when the body was taken away. It took quite a while as the archaeologist spent considerable time taking photographs and soil samples before allowing us to remove what was left. So I took some photos myself. One of them showed what looked like a rusty bottle top stuck to some old clothing. But when I enlarged it there appeared to be a clear image of a few lines and some writing. I might be mistaken, but it looked to me very much like one of the CND peace badges some people still wear today. I don't have to tell you that, if I am right, the remains could well belong to someone who has died sometime during the last fifty or sixty years.'

'What is happening at the site now?' DCS Sutton asked.

'We have cordoned off a substantial section and told the contractors they cannot continue their work until we have the report from the forensic archaeologist.'

'What about security?' Steve asked, thinking about what he learnt from Mick Mendham.

'We have an officer guarding the actual excavation until Monday afternoon by which time we hope to know a bit more.'

'Great,' Steve replied, 'please tell him or her to expect a visit from me later today.'

After the conversation had finished DCS Sutton looked at Steve.

'What's the hurry?'

'Nothing really, but I'm off to see my dad and was planning to visit the site anyway,' he explained before relating to her what he found out during Mick Mendham's visit earlier in the week.

Chapter 5

It had been a week since Councillor Anthony Fisher met Bob Bradley at the golf club to discuss the issue of the protesters outside the proposed New Town development. Since then everything had remained quiet and Fisher sincerely hoped it was going to stay that way. He and his wife were getting ready to attend the annual dinner and dance at the golf course. The event was supposed to be non-political but in reality all the councillors attending belonged to the party in power on Black Fen Drove District Council. At the dinner they would be joined by party supporters as well as a number of the wealthier landowners and businessmen in the area. It was a major event in the social calendar and Anthony was looking forward to doing some networking and extending his list of useful contacts. While he was thinking about this, Saskia, his wife, walked into the room and asked his opinion on her choice of dress for the evening.

'You look stunning,' he told her and meant every

word of it. She was wearing a simple black dress, understated high heels and a grey designer jacket which complemented the tone and colour of her hair. He was a lucky man, he realised. Not only was this beautiful woman his wife, she would also be a real asset when it came to talking to some of the more powerful men at the dinner tonight.

After saying goodbye to his colleagues Steve got in his car and headed south on the A10. He had rung ahead and told his father that he was going to be a little later than promised as he was visiting the airfield first. Before long he reached the entrance to the golf club. He could see plenty of expensive looking cars in the car park but there was no sign of any demonstrators. However, as soon as he turned the corner at the end of the perimeter fence, he was once again stopped by a small group of protesters carrying similar placards to the ones he encountered a few days earlier. He slowed down and opened his window. This time a woman walked up to him and offered him a leaflet. He explained that he already had one and started to shut the window. Just when he was about to drive away the woman said,
  'Steve?'
He opened his window again, and looked at the person in front of him.

'Well I never,' he exclaimed, 'Anne Trevelyan, my word. How are you? How long has it been?'

'I thought it was you,' she replied. 'I suppose I shouldn't be surprised. Do your parents still live down here?'

'My dad does,' Steve explained but before he could go on he realised he was blocking the road.

'Listen Anne,' he said quickly, 'I can't stop now but here's my card. Give me a ring sometime and maybe we can have a catch up over a cup of tea.'

'I'll do that, that'll be great,' she replied.

Well, well, well Steve said to himself as he drove away. *Anne Trevelyan, now there's a blast from the past.* He remembered how Anne and he travelled together on the school bus to Ely every day for four years. She was a year older than him but that hadn't stopped them becoming, if not friends, good mates. After all, there weren't many other young people in this far flung corner of the fens. He recalled his father telling him that she got married not long after she finished her 'A levels' but that the marriage had not worked out. The last thing he heard was that she had become a teacher. Not surprising really, seeing that her father had been the headmaster of the local primary school. *Of course, her father.* He now remembered the elderly gentleman who had spoken to him on the previous demonstration; Anne's father.

His trip down memory lane was soon interrupted when he reached the gate close to where the body had been found. Two police cars were present. Steve parked, got out and walked towards the open gate. He was greeted by a woman in her mid-thirties.

'Detective Sergeant Mary Ledbetter,' she introduced herself. 'How can I help you?'

Steve explained who he was after which DS Ledbetter guided him towards an area cordoned off with blue and white tape. The police officer guarding the scene helpfully lifted the tape and gathered the tarpaulin which had been used to cover the exact spot.

What they were looking at was a hole, roughly six feet square and six feet deep. It was clear from the smooth surface that the bottom of the hole had been carefully examined by the scene of crime officers. As a result there was very little of any interest left to see.

'So this is where they found him?' Steve asked, addressing DS Ledbetter.

'It is,' she replied, 'and before you ask, we've not heard from forensics or the pathologist so at the moment we still have no idea who the unfortunate person was, or equally important, how he ended up here.'

'Any suggestion of foul play?' Steve asked.

'Not as far as I know …' she paused before continuing, 'this is pure speculation but the body was found at least two metres below the ground. That suggests to me that it was buried here.'

'Good point,' agreed Steve. 'I suppose we'll have to wait until the results of the autopsy. Any idea when that might be?'

'I've been promised Monday afternoon at two o'clock. I won't be able to go myself but if you wish, feel free to attend. I suppose, depending on the outcome, your boss will have to talk to mine about who is going to take this case further if necessary.' Steve nodded.

'As soon as we have some more details we'll have to do a missing persons search.'

DS Ledbetter took out her phone and showed Steve the picture of the badge found near the body. He agreed it looked like the peace symbol used by CND.

'This could be very useful in establishing roughly when he died,' he responded.

While talking they'd slowly walked back to the gate. They said goodbye to the officer on duty and got in their cars. Steve continued on the road around the perimeter fence until he got to the compound where a number of tractors, diggers and such like were parked. He recognised Mick Mendham's logo on some of the equipment. Nothing seemed to be out of order. He turned his car around and took a final look in his rear view mirror. Just then a man with a camera stepped out from behind a hut and took a photo of Steve's car. Steve reversed and introduced himself to the stranger who was looking at him suspiciously. He relaxed when he realised that Steve was a police officer. It turned out he was the security guard. Steve was impressed. At least this guy was proactive. He shook his hand and got back in his car. It had been quite a busy hour and a half. He was actually getting a little tired so he was pleased that before long his father's farm appeared in the distance.

Chapter 6

Councillor Fisher was enjoying the meal. The chef had surpassed himself and he had trouble not going back to get a second helping of the excellent fish pie. But to do so would look greedy, and anyway, he had to watch his waistline.

There was a small lull in proceedings while the room was rearranged for the dancing to start. The musicians were tuning their instruments, the waiters were clearing up the plates and most of the guests had gathered on the veranda overlooking the golf course.

Anthony stepped away from the crowd and lit a cigarette. He was thinking about the speeches. Most of them had been about the new development with the majority of the guests strongly in favour. But he was surprised when Arthur Turner, one of the older members of the party, had stood up and discussed the proposals in slightly less favourable language. Was it sour grapes? After all Arthur Turner had sold the land to Future Build which now stood to make a tidy profit if the development went ahead. But surely not. Turner had done well out of the deal and was by all accounts a millionaire several times over. Still it was puzzling. Just then the man he had been thinking about approached him.

'Councillor Fisher, I would like a few minutes of your time. Do you mind if I join you?'

Without waiting for an answer Arthur Turner produced a cigar from a beautiful wooden case.

'I'm glad you're here. I've been planning to talk to you for quite some time.'

'I'm honoured,' Anthony replied, wondering where this was going.

'Let me explain,' Turner continued through a cloud of smoke. 'As you probably know, I have been around a long time. It was my company that originally bought this site from the Ministry of Defence and developed the golf club. I am also one of the founder members of the local party branch you represent on Black Fen Drove District Council.'

He paused, flicking the ash of his cigar on the floor.

'I have followed your rise through the ranks with interest and very much approve of most of the policies and causes you support. I think, and I am not alone in this, that you have the ability and personality to go far. As a matter of fact I can easily see why some are mentioning you as a possible prospective parliamentary candidate.'

Anthony couldn't believe his ears. Tonight was going better than he ever could have hoped for. He was about to say something when Turner continued in a slightly different, quieter tone of voice.

'But, and I'm sure you understand this, you must be very careful not to do anything that might diminish your chances in front of the selection panel of which I, I'm sure you know, am the Chairman.'

Anthony started to feel uncomfortable. *Where is this leading?* He didn't have to wait long.

'Now I understand that you are one of the main proponents of driving this New Town development forward. As you may have deduced from my speech, I'm not entirely happy with the plans.'

'Why not?' Anthony heard himself asking.

'Many different reasons, most of which don't concern you. Let's just say that I think this is not the right place for such a large scale development.'

This is bullshit, Anthony realised.

'Why are you telling me this,' he asked.

'You've got a bright future ahead of you,' replied Turner. 'If I were you I'd think carefully who you side with over the next few months. You wouldn't want your support for this development to jeopardise your career prospects now, would you?'

And with that he chucked the remainder of his cigar over the veranda and walked away, leaving Anthony alone with his thoughts. He lit another cigarette and then looked around, trying to find Saskia. Suddenly he'd had enough and wanted to go home. Saskia would know what to do but before he could see her he felt a tap on his shoulder.

'Mr Fisher, could you come with me please, Mr Bradley needs to see you. It's urgent,' the steward told him.

What now? Anthony thought to himself, *it's nearly ten o'clock, what can be so urgent at this time of the evening?*

But of course he followed the steward who led him to a small conference room, showed him in and then withdrew. Anthony was surprised to find not only Bob Bradley in the room but also Arthur Turner. It looked as if the two men had been arguing.

'What's up?' he asked, trying to keep his voice sounding jovial.

'I think we've got a problem,' Bob Bradley replied. 'Did you know there was another demonstration tonight near the east perimeter fence?'

Before Anthony could answer Arthur Turner cut in.

'Never mind the demonstration. What about the body? I told you no good would come from you developing that site.'

Bob Bradley was turning red.

'All I know is that finding that body is going to cause considerable delay and who's paying for it all? I am.'

Anthony was taken aback.

'What are you talking about?' he asked neither of the two men in particular. 'Who has found a body?'

Bob Bradley quickly filled him in on the details.

'But surely, some old skeleton won't cause that long a delay,' he responded.

'I hope it does', replied Arthur Turner looking straight at Anthony. 'I've made it clear that I'm not in favour of this development and I suggest both of you think carefully about how you proceed from now on.'

And with that he stormed out of the room.

'What was all that about?' Anthony asked.

'I've no idea,' Bob Bradley replied. 'He's been against the idea from the beginning. I think it's sour grapes that he didn't think of it himself before he sold the land to us.'

Anthony was not so sure. He had to find Saskia and tell her everything he's learnt tonight and see what she thinks!

Chapter 7

When Steve walked into the station on Monday morning Maddie was waiting for him.

'Before you go upstairs could you just go to the holding cells? I think Sergeant Newman can do with some help. He's got an elderly gentleman down there.'

'No worries,' Steve replied and made his way to the corridor where the cells were. Before he got there he could hear a voice loudly addressing Sergeant Newman.

'I don't care who you are. I want to speak to the organ grinder, not the monkey.'

Sergeant Newman sighed and then noticed Steve.

'Thank God you're here sir, this is Mr Evans. He is not happy with the way ……'

Before he could finish his sentence Mr Evans interrupted.

'Are you in charge?' Without waiting for an answer he continued, 'Can you tell your underling to release me from custody and let me go home so I can start writing a formal complaint about the way I have been treated.'

'Let's just calm down a minute Mr Evans,' Steve replied. 'I will be with you in a minute. Sergeant, can you come with me please and explain what's been happening.'

When out of earshot of the still complaining Mr Evans, Sergeant Newman explained to Steve that the gentleman in question had called 999 earlier that morning and asked for the police as he believed there was an intruder in his house. When two officers arrived a short time later they had found Mr Evans waiting for them in the front garden.

'He's in the kitchen,' he had greeted them. 'Please arrest him and tell him not to come back.'

The officers had carefully made their way to the kitchen where they found a man sitting at a table, reading the newspaper and drinking a cup of tea. When they'd asked him what he was doing in Mr Evan's house, the man had explained that he lived there. At that point Mr Evans had entered the room and shouted.

'There he is, take him away. He is not welcome here.'

It was clear to the officers that they had walked in on a domestic dispute between father and son. They had rung for advice and were told that unless either party was in danger they should return to the station. When they told Mr Evans that this was not a police matter he had become abusive and as a result they had taken him to the station and put him in a cell to calm down.

Steve thanked Sergeant Newman and returned to Mr Evans.

'Come with me,' he suggested, 'we'll go to my office and have some coffee, or tea if you prefer.'

By the time they sat down Mr Evans had calmed down.

'I'm sorry I lost my temper with your colleagues,' he told Steve, 'but I've simply had enough. I just want that lay-about out of my house.'

'What exactly is the problem?' Steve asked.

Mr Evans explained that he was eighty-three years old and that his wife had died a year earlier. His three children had all attended the funeral. Two of them, he said, lived "good lives" and had gone back home afterwards but the youngest, his fifty-three year old son, had stayed on, on the pretence that he was going to look after his father.

'Him,' he cried out, 'look after me! He can't even look after himself. He's never done a day's work in his life and now he sees the chance to scrounge off me for the rest of my life.'

'When you say he can't even look after himself,' Steve interrupted gently, 'do you mean he's got mental health problems?'

'That's exactly what I mean,' Mr Evans replied.

'He's a socialist.'

Steve smiled to himself when he recounted the story to DCS Sutton later on.

'I mean,' he explained, 'I know we live in a rather conservative area, but I've never heard that being a socialist is the same as having a mental illness.'

'Where is Mr Evans now?' Sarah asked.

'We gave him a lift back home and Maddie has referred him to a social worker from Age Concern.'

'Well let's hope that's it and they work it out between them,' Sarah replied.

Steve finished his coffee and made his way back to his office. Just as he sat down his phone pinged. It was a message from Anne asking if Steve was free later that afternoon. Before he had a chance to answer he got another message, this time from DS Ledbetter, informing him that the autopsy had been brought forward to twelve o'clock and asking if he was going to attend. Steve looked at the clock and realised he had ample time to get to Cambridge before then. He replied that he would indeed make his way to the mortuary where the autopsy was taking place before texting Anne that, as luck would have it, he would be driving through Ely sometime between three and four o'clock.

Chapter 8

At the same time Steve was remonstrating with Mr Evans, Councillor Fisher was on his way to a meeting with Bob Bradley. It seemed appropriate that they were meeting back at the golf club. Anthony felt positive. As a matter of fact he was determined not to let Bob Bradley, or Arthur Turner or anyone else, spoil his mood. He'd actually put his golf clubs in the back of his Mercedes. If the meeting finished by lunchtime he might even get a round in.

He had been right of course, Saskia knew what to do. Again he can't stop himself from thinking how lucky he was to have met such an incredible woman. They had arrived back at their house late on Friday night and while Saskia opened a bottle of wine Anthony had told her all about the events of the evening. Saskia had listened carefully, only interrupting him when something wasn't clear to her.

'Let me think about all this,' she had told him when the clock indicated that it was way past midnight.

'The best thing we can do is get some sleep and look at it again in the morning when we are both refreshed.'

Anthony had agreed and was surprised how well he had slept when he went down for breakfast the next morning. But rather than the smell of bacon and eggs which had become a weekend tradition for them, he found Saskia engrossed on her computer. He had stood looking at her for a few minutes before asking,

'How long have you been up?'

'Long enough to have earned a posh breakfast in town,' she'd replied and with that she had shut her laptop lid and winked at him.

'You drive, just park anywhere near the cathedral.'

The Almonry, next to Ely Cathedral, wasn't necessarily the poshest restaurant in town but it was open and did a range of croissants and cakes to die for. The weather was great so they decided to sit outside in the pleasant gardens with a view of the cathedral itself. Although Anthony was eager to hear what Saskia had to say, he knew better than to push her. She had obviously come up with a solution and he decided to wait. By the time the waiter had brought her a second latte she was ready to discuss her thoughts.

'So the problem as I see it is that Arthur Turner

wants you to stop supporting the development and Bob Bradley needs you to get the whole thing through the planning process. And you have to make a choice?'

'That's more or less it,' he agreed before adding, 'but there's also the body and the protests.'

'Forget about those things for a moment, they just cloud the waters. We've got to decide which of the two parties are most beneficial to you and therefore to me as well.'

He loved her direct style; she didn't mince her words but immediately got to the heart of the matter.

'Well,' she had smiled, 'it's easy really. Arthur Turner wants you to do something of no interest to us while Bob Bradley needs you and stands to make us significant financial gains. So it's a no brainer really.'

'But what about Arthur Turner's influence on the party and the selection process?'

'Who cares,' she had replied. 'Turner is an old man. If you don't get nominated now you will be in five years, by which time he'll be dead and the New Town development will have proved a success. What a shame they don't serve champagne here at this time of the morning. I'd like to toast our future together.'

While turning into the carpark at the golf club his thoughts turned again to Saskia, They had returned home where she insisted they go back to bed and they had made love with the windows and blinds wide open. He loved her, he admired her, in fact, he was in awe of her. But he also realised that occasionally, just occasionally, he was just a little bit scared of her.

When Steve arrived at the large building which housed the mortuary in Cambridge he was met by DS Ledbetter.

'I thought you weren't able to make it,' Steve greeted her.

'I wasn't,' she replied, 'but in light of the initial findings my boss has asked me to move my diary around a bit.'

'Initial findings?' Steve enquired.

'Yes, we were contacted earlier by the forensic archaeologist who told us that the body in question had been in the ground most likely less than thirty years. As a result he had taken the initiative to ask our regular pathologist to attend.'

They entered the building and were guided to a large room on the first floor where they were greeted by the two experts. The body was laid out on a marble slab and a technician was busy putting all the equipment in the right place.

Steve and DS Ledbetter were asked to sit down after which the archaeologist picked up a microphone and described what he saw before him. He pointed out that clothes and soil samples were in the process of being analysed but that the results would take a few days to come through.

'However,' he concluded, 'looking at the stage of decomposition, coupled with some of the clothes fragments found on the body, I would say that we are discussing a relatively recent death.'

Steve was not used to such a quick and definite opinion.

'What makes you so sure?' he asked.

The archaeologist smiled and walked over to a table where a number of evidence bags were placed. He picked one of them up and handed it to Steve.

'This,' he said. Inside the evidence bag was a relatively modern digital wristwatch.

'I've done some quick research and discovered that this particular model has only been available since 1995. We are therefore fairly certain that our body has been in the ground for less than twenty-seven years. He turned to the pathologist.

'Ms Carver, would you like to take it from here?'

'Thank you, I will.'

Addressing the two detectives she continued.

'I agree with my colleague that we are talking about a relatively recent burial here. What we need to determine is the cause of death in order to establish if a crime was involved or not. And just like my colleague I am happy to give you an initial opinion which is that the evidence suggests that the man's death was the result of at least two blows to the head.'

She walked over to the table and asked the detectives to join her. She pointed to a part of the skull which had obviously been crushed.

'Could that not have happened by accident, maybe when he fell?' Steve asked.

'Theoretically that is possible but he would have had to hit a hard object like a stone or something like it. My colleague assured me that the soil around the body was relatively soft and that there was no evidence of rock or other hard matter in the vicinity. But the real reason I suspect the poor man was murdered is because there is further damage elsewhere.'

She pointed to a small indent a few inches away from the spot where the skull had been crushed.

'It has obviously been caused by another blow to the head, most likely from a crowbar or hammer. It has left an imprint but I can't for the life of me work out exactly what was used to cause that.'

The detectives got closer and, using a magnifying glass, could clearly see a number of lines imprinted on the skull.

'I will of course carry out a thorough further investigation and let you know if anything else comes up. But I thought you'd like to hear our initial findings as soon as possible.'

'Thank you very much,' said DS Ledbetter. 'We'll keep an open mind until we receive your final report but at least we can start with trying to identify the poor victim. Is there any other information you can give us that might be useful?'

'Well,' Ms Carver replied, 'my colleague and I talked about this. We both think the body is that of a male in his mid-twenties. He was just under two metres tall and had very good teeth. This fact might actually hinder identification on the basis of dental records. My colleague suggests that he was dressed casually, t-shirt and shorts. We have to confirm this of course but if this is the case, he probably died when the weather was reasonably warm so most likely between May and the end of September. As for the timeframe of his death I would suggest sometime between 1995 and 2000.'

'This is really useful,' said Steve. 'What about personal belongings?'

'Not much,' answered the archaeologist. 'Apart

from the badge you know about already, the only other thing we found was a key which we believe to be from a bicycle lock.'

'Thank you,' replied Steve. 'Like I said this is really useful and will give us a good start with the identification process.'

'Thank you,' Ms Carver answered, 'but please remember, these are our initial findings only. We may find out more or we may have to discard some of the suggestions and opinions we've voiced today.'

Outside DS Ledbetter suggested a coffee to which Steve happily agreed. Once they were seated with two cappuccinos, and in Steve's case, a fruit scone, DS Ledbetter got straight to the point.

'I suppose the next step is missing persons. But I've been told by my boss not to commit too many officers to this case. In fact, he suggested we ask your unit to take the lead here. According to him we have enough to do without taking on historic crimes.'

Steve smiled. He was aware that some other forces were not always sure what the Special Fenland Police Force actually did and as a result, believed that they had an easy time of it.

'No worries,' he replied, 'we'd be happy to take the lead. After all, we're not doing much else at the moment.'

DS Ledbetter looked at him in surprise. Was he being sarcastic? She decided not to inquire.

'That's great. I'll be your liaison with our force. Call me if you think there is anything we can do to assist you.' With that she finished her coffee, got up and left for her car.

It was only after she had gone that Steve realised that rather than being sarcastic he had actually spoken the truth. For the last month or so they had done very little case work indeed.

Chapter 9

While Steve was on his way back from Cambridge, Alan Phelan, the editor and senior journalist of the Fenland Gazette, sat in his office enjoying a cup of coffee while checking the news feed that had arrived over the weekend. Another demonstration at the site of the proposed New Town development, a report on the dinner and dance at the golf club and Saturday's local sports results. Nothing out of the ordinary but enough to get on with and start preparing tomorrow's edition. He just caught a newsflash on the Cambridgeshire police internet page indicating that a body had been found near the airfield when he was interrupted by his secretary who told him there was a gentleman hoping to see him.

'What is it about?' he asked.

'I'm not sure,' she replied, 'but I recognise him as a Green Party councillor.'

'He'll be after some free publicity. Tell him to email me the story or make an appointment.'

She disappeared but returned almost immediately.

'He says he's not here with a story, rather he needs your advice.'

Odd, Alan thought to himself but as he was intrigued he asked his secretary to take the visitor to the conference room.

'Oh, and see if he wants anything to drink.'

The man in front of him introduced himself as Richard Evans. Alan guessed he must be somewhere in his mid-fifties. He was casually dressed and it was clear that he was fit and had looked after himself.

'Good afternoon,' Alan welcomed him, 'I understand you are a Green Party councillor.'

'I am indeed,' replied Mr Evans, 'but that's not why I'm here. I want to talk to you about something but I'm not sure where to start.'

'Please, take your time.'

By now both men were seated and momentarily quiet as Alan's secretary brought in a tray with coffee and biscuits.

'The thing is,' Mr Evans continued, 'I was going over it in my head last night and thought it might be a good idea to talk to someone. But now that I'm here it sort of sounds a bit stupid.'

'Why don't you start at the beginning,' Alan suggested.

'Okay, as you know I am now a respectable Green Party councillor. I also work part-time as a solicitor at the local advice centre in Wisbech. What you might not know is that I have spent most of my life campaigning on environmental issues, both here and abroad. As such I have met a lot of people, not only activists, but also lawyers, businessmen and politicians from all sides of the political spectrum. I have always been very cautious in my dealings with people I don't know as I am careful not to have my credibility questioned or undermined. So for example, we were once offered a large sum of money by one of the oil companies who wanted to improve their green credentials. I fought hard to refuse it.' He paused.

Interesting, Alan thought to himself, *but where is this going?*

'Anyway,' Mr Evans continued, 'I'll get to the point. While working at the advice centre I was approached by a few locals who knew about my background and asked me to join them in setting up a group campaigning against the proposed New Town development. I took some time studying the facts and decided this was something I was happy to get involved in. We had a few meetings and decided that the group should be independent from other pressure groups and political parties as this is very much a single issue campaign. Part of that means that we agreed to be self-financing, maybe have the occasional benefit concert if we needed some cash for renting mini buses or printing flyers and so on. We've now been active for about a month and so far so good. We had a good turnout at the two demonstrations we've held at the site. Lots of people have asked for more information. Then on Saturday, I received this.' He took a piece of paper out of his pocket and showed it to Alan. It was a copy of an email and read:

Dear Mr Evans, I am very much in favour of your opposition to the proposed New Town development. I do think however that your campaign so far has not caused enough impact and wonder if this is because you lack the funds to really hit the headlines. For that purpose I would like to donate £10,000 to you personally for your cause. This will allow you to step up the campaign and pay for possible police fines etc. To ensure my anonymity in this matter I will make this donation in cash.

Yours,
A supporter

Alan handed the piece of paper back to Mr Evans.
'And?' he asked.

'This arrived this morning in my letterbox.' Out of his rucksack Mr Evans produced a large bag full of money.

'I've counted it. It's £10,000 exactly,' he said.

Alan was rather perplexed.

'Why haven't you gone to the police?' he enquired.

'That was my first thought but when I started thinking about it I realised they would not be interested, after all no crime has been committed. Also, my father and I are not on the best of terms with the local officers.'

He smiled and related what had happened earlier that morning.

'What do the other members of your group think?'

'I haven't told them yet. I'm worried they'll get over excited and want to start spending the money without thinking of the consequences.'

'What consequences?'

'Nobody hands over £10,000 without expecting a return. What I've learnt is that once you accept this kind of support they, whoever they are, have you in the palm of their hands.'

'So why come to me?'

'I thought that with your local knowledge you might help me find out who the donor is. You never know, it might even make a good story.'

'Let me think about it,' Alan replied, 'you might be right, it could make a good story.'

'What shall I do in the meantime?' Mr Evans asked.

'I suggest you make sure the money is put in a safe place.'

'I have a bank safety deposit box in Peterborough, I could put it there.'

'Excellent idea,' Alan replied. 'Secondly I would reply to the email, acknowledge the receipt of the cash and say that you will speak to your fellow campaigners in due course. That will buy you some time. Oh, and ask him or her if you can meet up. You never know. If you leave your details at the front desk I'll be in touch as soon as I've made up my mind about the whole thing.'

'Thanks,' replied Mr Evans, 'I feel better now that I've told you.'

Alan watched him leave. *Why,* he wondered, *does a part time solicitor and activist need a bank safety deposit box?*

Chapter 10

Just as he was leaving the café Steve's phone pinged. It was another message from Anne. He had told her he would be driving through Ely that afternoon and would be pleased to meet up. He rang back immediately and they agreed to meet at the coffee place on the market square.

Unusually the A10 from Cambridge to Ely was clear so Steve arrived with half an hour to spare. He decided to have a quick look in the cathedral. He had visited many times before but never tired of observing the craftsmanship that had gone into this magnificent building. He was also aware that whenever he sat down and the only sound around him were the hushed voices of tourists he soon relaxed. Steve was not a religious man but he was happy to admit that a place like this definitely had a spiritual dimension. But today the purpose of his visit was to see the new table which had been recently installed. Made out of bog oak found in a field near Downham Market, the wood was several thousand years old. He had seen pictures of it on the local news but he couldn't believe his eyes when he saw it for himself. Not only was the table enormous and would easily seat fifty people, it was also absolutely beautiful. *I must bring Dad to see this, he thought to himself. I'm sure he'd appreciate it.* It was obvious to Steve that the skills of those craftsmen who built the cathedral over a thousand years ago were still present today. This thought somehow cheered him up.

He looked at his watch and realised he'd better make a move or Anne might think he wasn't coming. He took a short cut through the cathedral gardens, crossed the High Street and arrived at the Market Place. Tables, chairs and sun umbrellas were scattered around a mobile coffee truck. He looked around and spotted Anne coming out of a covered walkway. She had seen him and joined him in the queue. They ordered their coffees and found a table out of the sun. They looked at each other, both slightly apprehensive and not sure where to start. After all it was nearly thirty years since they last saw each other and at that time they were teenagers.

'It's good to see you again,' Steve started. 'I think the last time I saw you was during all the protests against the proposal for storing nuclear waste at the old airfield.'

'Those were the days,' she replied. 'So what have you been doing with yourself? Last I heard you had joined the police force.'

'I did and I'm still in it. I joined the Met in London but came back a few years ago. I'm now based in Downham Market. What about you? I was told you'd become a teacher.'

'That's right,' Anne replied. 'As a matter of fact, I've recently been appointed Headteacher at the same primary school where my dad used to work. I suppose it's not half as exciting as your job must be?'

'Oh, I don't know,' Steve answered. 'I'm sure we both spend a great deal of our time on unnecessary paperwork.'

'I agree with you there,' Anne laughed before continuing somewhat hesitantly,

'And what about yourself, do you have a family?'

'I have two teenage boys, they live in London with their mother. We're separated,' he added. 'What about you?'

'I have a son,' Anne replied, 'he's an adult now really. He's just finished university. His father and I split up when he was four so I've brought him up alone.'

'That must have been hard.'

'It's the reason I became a teacher. Regular hours and no problems finding someone to take care of him during the school holidays. It's why I moved back in with my parents so my mum could look after him while I commuted to Bedford to get my teaching qualification.'

'How are your parents?'

'They're well. Mum has a little trouble with her hips but Dad's doing fine. They live in Peterborough now.'

Steve told Anne that he recognised her dad at the demonstration.

'I know,' she said. 'Isn't it strange how people change? You remember the protests twenty-five years ago? He didn't have a good word to say about any of the people who took part at the time and now look at him. Handing out leaflets, blocking roads. I told him he owes me an apology for coming down so hard on me when he found out I secretly visited the demonstrations all those years ago.'

They chatted about old times for a while then Anne looked at her watch.

'Gosh, is that the time? I'd better get back before Paul, that's my son, thinks I've had an accident.'

'So he still lives with you?'

'Not really. On and off. Just while he's trying to decide what to do with the rest of his life.' They both stood up to go.

'Perhaps we could meet up again, if you'd like to?'

'I'd like that,' Anne replied. 'Call me, you've got my number.'

While driving back to Downham Market Steve reflected on the time he had just spent with Anne. Yes it had been a little awkward at first but that soon disappeared. He had to admit that he'd really enjoyed himself and that, if he was honest, he wouldn't mind seeing her again soon.

Chapter 11

Bob Bradley was seriously pissed off. Those were the words he had used earlier in the day when talking to Anthony Fisher about his problems. The work had stopped since the body was found, planning had not been officially approved, the protesters had been back, Mick Mendham had been bending his ear about compensation for his damaged diggers and now he had been called to a meeting with one of the major shareholders in his company, Future Build.

'I don't know what you want me to do about it.' Anthony had said. 'After all, I can't bring the planning meeting forward because that would look suspicious and anyhow, without the report on the soil testing, the committee won't consider the proposal anyway.'

It left Bob Bradley in a quandary. The soil tests themselves had been completed but they needed to keep the inspection holes open in case members of building control wanted to have another look. That was planned for this week but now the site was cordoned off. He got his jacket and made his way to his car to drive to Peterborough where he was meeting Derk Pieters who owned nearly fifty percent of the shares in the company and therefore was more or less the boss.

Bradley doesn't like Pieters, there's something about him he doesn't trust. And then there's the fact that Pieters is a foreigner. True, South Africa was part of the Commonwealth and Pieters had settled in England, but in Bob Bradley's mind he was still a foreigner. And Mr Bradley doesn't like foreigners. As far as he was concerned everybody should stay where they were born. *Foreignland,* as he called it, was a place to visit and have a good time. Soak up the sun and be waited on hand and foot by smiling Spanish teenagers while watching good-looking tanned senoritas. Why did they want to come over here anyway? He got himself more and more worked up so by the time he arrived at the Great Northern Hotel, where they had agreed to meet, the first thing Derk Pieters said, while they were shaking hands, was, 'are you alright? You look as if you're about to have a heart attack.'

'Don't worry,' Bradley replied, 'I'll be fine once I've got a drink in me.' The two men made their way to the terrace.

'I'll come straight to the point,' said Pieters. 'I'm a little concerned about the amount of money we're spending on this New Town development without seeing any sign that we can start building soon.'

Bob Bradley took a sip of his whiskey and lit a cigarette. This gave him time to think.

'Under normal circumstances I'd agree with you,' he said. 'But I'm not sure that you know exactly what we're up against.'

He continued by telling Pieters about the site being cordoned off by the police, the protesters, and Arthur Turner making a nuisance of himself.

'I see,' Pieters said reassuringly. 'That must be irritating to say the least. But you're sure you've got it all under control and we are not going to have any further surprises at the planning committee stage?'

'Don't worry,' Bradley said, secretly relieved. 'I've got Councillor Fisher in the palm of my hand. When I say jump, he asks how high.'

'That's good to know,' Pieters replied, 'and are you sure you are still the right person to lead this company?'

Without waiting for a response he got up and went inside leaving Bradley sitting on the terrace, confused, angry and not a little bit scared. Was that last question a threat?

While Bob Bradley was getting hot under the collar, Steve and his team were meeting in the incident room at the police station. As he looked around at Detective Chief Superintendent Sarah Sutton, Detective Inspector Simon Woods and Detective Sergeant Dave Newman, they were joined by Eva Lappinska in her new role as Detective Constable. They all knew her from the previous case when she was attached to the team but DCS Sutton made a point of formally welcoming her as part of the family. The others all clapped before Sarah asked Steve to update everyone on what had been happening so far. He quickly went over the major points and then turned to his meeting with the pathologist and the archaeologist the day before.

'There's little doubt in their minds,' he explained, 'that our victim died of unnatural causes, most likely a blow to the head. Even though this was probably over twenty-five years ago, we must treat it for what it is: a murder enquiry. After all, the perpetrator of this crime is most likely still living somewhere in the area. Who knows what else he or she has got up to? So to start we must try and find out the identity of the victim as soon as possible. Eva, I've arranged with DS Ledbetter for you to go to Cambridge and examine missing person reports in the area between 1995 and 2001. Concentrate on males between sixteen and forty for a start.'

'Can't Eva work from here?' Sarah Sutton asked.

'She can, but not all records have been transferred to digital files yet so we will have to do some old-fashioned paper searches.' Eva nodded.

'I'll give her a ring and make an appointment,' she said.

'Good. Simon, I would like you to do some research into the background and the people involved in the protests of 1996. If our victim was one of the protesters we will probably need that information. After all, where he was found, as well as the CND badge, suggests he may have been one of the activists. I myself have made an appointment to see Alan Phelan at the Fenland Gazette. He was a young reporter at the time and may well remember something. Any questions?'

None were forthcoming and with that they all returned to their desks and offices. Steve accompanied Eva to her desk.

'So how do you feel?' he asked.

She looked him directly in the eye and replied,

'Honestly, I can't wait to get stuck in.'

Alan Phelan has had a difficult night. He kept thinking about the conversation he'd had with his visitor, Richard Evans. He recalled the moment Mr Evans produced the bag stuffed with banknotes, more cash than Alan had ever seen in his life. But he had come to a decision. He's rung Richard Evans and told him he was happy to do some investigating but from the point of view of a possible news story rather than on behalf of Mr Evans.

'And if I find that anything illegal is going on, you realise I will have to tell the police.'

'Of course,' came the reply. 'The same goes for me. Thank you, I'll keep you informed of what's happening on my side. By the way, I replied to the email but it bounced back.' He paused. 'There's something else. Please tell me if I'm being paranoid, but whoever put the money in my letterbox knows where I live and I can't help feeling as if I'm being watched.'

'I'm not surprised,' Alan agreed. 'I would no doubt feel worried myself.'

With that he rang off. Just then his secretary called him and asked if he was able to fit DCI Culverhouse in for a quick chat.

'I'll always make time for the law,' Alan greeted Steve. 'What can I do for you?'

'I wonder what you remember of the protests in 1996 at the old airbase?' Steve asked.

'Quite a lot as it happens. It was one of the first stories I reported on as a young journalist. It was exciting really, lots of exotic people from all over the country setting up camp and mixing with the locals. Is this to do with the body you've found?'

'We're not sure at the moment,' Steve replied. 'I must ask you not to publish anything about it other than the facts for the time being.'

Alan nodded and Steve continued.

'Do you remember who the prominent players were at the time?'

'I think it was very much a case of the Atomic Energy Council against Friends of the Earth and CND. Oh, and there was of course Arthur Turner who owned the site and was trying to get planning permission for nuclear waste storage.'

'Were there any scuffles or fights, I mean did it ever become nasty or violent?'

'Not that I can remember; a lot of it was good-natured banter during the demonstrations. But I do remember that some of the locals got quite annoyed that the police did nothing to remove the protesters.'

Steve smiled. He remembered his father coming home one day explaining he'd been held up for three hours because some demonstrators had blocked the road.

'I'll tell you what I'll do,' Alan continued, 'it's a bit embarrassing but like I said it was one of my first big stories so I kept all the articles I wrote. I've got a scrapbook at home. If you're interested I'll drop it off at the station on my way to work tomorrow. As long as I get it back.'

'I'll take good care of it,' Steve promised. 'That could be really useful.'

Chapter 12

Anthony Fisher was on his way to *The Carpenters Arms*, a lovely country pub close to Downham Market. He had arranged to meet some of the key members of the planning committee away from the council offices in Black Fen Drove. When he arrived the others were already there. He had rung the landlady beforehand and reserved a table in a small room, away from the main bar and restaurant.

'Before we start,' he asked, 'what does everyone want to drink?'

'Blimey,' said one of his fellow councillors, 'that's the first time I've seen you buy a round. Are you trying to bribe us or something?'

They all laughed, including Anthony, even though he was acutely aware that that was exactly what he was planning to do. Once the drinks were in, the questions began.

'As much as I like going to the pub, can I ask why we are meeting here, rather than at the council office?' asked the councillor nearest to him.

'Simple,' replied Anthony, 'I wanted to sound you out informally about something before we have our planned official meeting. You know how some of the staff gossip so if we had met at base no doubt one or two members of the committee might have felt left out because they were not invited. And you know my mantra, always write the minutes before the meeting has started. That way you get what you want. I don't think I'm wrong in presuming that all four of us here are roughly of the same opinion when it comes to the direction of planning in our district. That includes a successful outcome of the New Town planning application. You are all probably aware that we have hit a snag with this body being discovered and that, as a result, the technical report is likely to be late which means we can't consider the application for another six weeks.'

'Does that matter?' one of them asked. 'Surely six weeks' delay on such a large project makes little difference?'

'Not to you or me maybe,' replied Anthony, 'but for Future Build and its associates, we're talking about a loss of several thousand pounds for each day the start of the project is delayed.'

'But I can't see how we can do anything about that,' replied the same councillor. 'The rules are very strict and without a technical report we won't be able to come to a decision.'

'That's not entirely true,' Anthony replied. 'I have consulted an independent lawyer on the matter and in exceptional circumstances a decision can be made in principle before all evidence has been considered, providing those reports are included as soon as they become available.'

Two of the other councillors shared a knowing look. They were well aware that the "independent lawyer" was no doubt Saskia, Councillor Fisher's wife.

'Be that as it may,' one of the councillors said, 'it still doesn't sit easy with me. What if we grant planning permission and the technical report throws something up which means we shouldn't have done so?'

'Don't worry,' Anthony replied, 'I can assure you that the technical report won't contain anything that might jeopardise the project. You have my word on that.' He got up. 'I'll just nip to the loo and get another round in, shall I? It will give you time to talk amongst yourselves.' He reached into his pocket.

'Oh, I nearly forgot. Bob Bradley has asked me to give you these in appreciation of all the work you've done supporting the project so far.'

He produced three envelopes with the golf club logo on the front page and handed one to each of his colleagues. The moment he had gone the three remaining men looked at each other.

'Surely he is not blatantly trying to bribe us,' one of them said. One of the others had opened his envelope. Inside was a brochure and an application form for membership of the golf club. It had already been filled in and all the men needed to do was sign the form. They started reading the information. When it came to the type of membership applied for it simply said:

"Complimentary Life Membership"

None of them spoke. By the time Anthony returned with the drinks, each of them had put their envelope away.

'So,' said Anthony, 'can I count on your support?'

'Don't worry,' said one of the men, 'there won't be any problems.' He raised his glass, 'Cheers everyone.'

Wednesday morning saw DC Eva Lappinska making her way back to Cambridge. She had decided to take the train to avoid the travel chaos she encountered near Ely the day before. Two lorries had collided. One had spread its load of carrots all over the carriageway. The other was transporting livestock and at least five pigs had escaped. Rather than running away they had soon made their way to the pile of carrots and had been happily munching away until a local farmer had arrived who, together with the driver, soon rounded them up. Comical as it was, it had been two hours before a replacement truck had arrived and Eva was keen to avoid a similar scenario today, hence the train.

She looked out of the window at the flat landscape all around her. Harvesting was just about to start and most fields were golden yellow. When the track crossed the road from Ten Mile Bank to Welney she remembered that she was going to ask Steve if he fancied going for a walk at the Wetland Centre this coming weekend. She had only just discovered it when out on one of her bike rides. Even though she wasn't particularly interested in birdwatching herself, she had nevertheless been impressed with the facilities on offer for those who were. And it offered some lovely walks, both in the reserve and on the riverbank. Also, she had to admit, the friendly service, yummy cakes and good coffee in the café were another excellent reason for a visit. She thought about the day ahead. Because of the traffic hold-up she had not really achieved much yesterday and she was determined to make up for it today. She relaxed and checked her notes.

Before long the train arrived at Cambridge Station and she made her way to the police headquarters. DS

Ledbetter had given her a desk to use for as long as she needed it. One of the uniformed officers had been assigned to show her where the records were kept. Before long she returned to her desk with three boxes full of files spanning the years 1995 to 1998. She had decided to start with 1996. If the theory that the victim was one of the protesters was correct this year would be the most relevant. She opened the file and found that it had a helpful index at the front. It appeared that a total of twenty-one people were reported missing in the Cambridge area during that year. Ten of them were women so she put those files to the side. Another six were over fifty years old so again she discarded those. This left her with five possible individuals. She knew that many of her colleagues thought this was a boring job but she couldn't help smiling. After all, this was the first time she had a real task in an investigation, rather than simply assisting other detectives. She went to the machine, got herself a coffee and settled down.

DI Simon Woods was back at the station conducting an internet search, trying to find as much information as possible on the protests back in 1996. He was bored. It was not that he thought what he was doing wasn't important but he was not keen on spending the whole day looking at a screen. He'd rather be out interviewing people, chasing criminals and, if it involved a car chase, so much the better. A twenty-five year old murder was hardly exciting as far as he was concerned. He yawned. *Better get on with it, I suppose,* he said to himself.

While DI Woods was trying to motivate himself downstairs, Steve was upstairs in his office, leafing through the three large scrapbooks Alan Phelan had brought in. Most of the articles simply reported on the obstruction caused by the protesters. One scrapbook was filled entirely with reports on the endless committee and council meetings held at the time. One article caught his eye. It was a double-page feature, written by Alan himself, in which he spent a day with the activists. A lot centred on mundane questions such as who cleaned the toilets, who did the cooking and where did they sleep. But it also contained a long article in which one of the protesters, William Gunn, explained why they were against the proposed nuclear dump. He cited several cases where similar facilities had led to increased cases of cancer and went into great depth about the chemical breakdown process of nuclear waste. Steve was not surprised to read further on that Mr Gunn had in fact worked as a chemistry lecturer at Imperial College in London. What really excited him was a photograph of several activists holding up placards and smiling at the camera. Helpfully, Alan Phelan had printed their names underneath. Steve checked the names and found that William Gunn was a tall man, probably in his late twenties, standing to the right of the others. He made a note of the other names, and took the file to Maddie, asking her to scan or copy the article.

Eva had whittled her files down to three on the basis that two of the five individuals were less than one metre sixty centimetres tall so couldn't possibly be the victim. By lunchtime she was ready for the last three files. All of them concerned young men, one in his late teens, the other two in their twenties. She had bought a sandwich on her way from the station so didn't have to go out for lunch.

She turned to the file of the teenager. Apparently he disappeared from his home in Cambridge the night before he was due to leave for university in London. He had been out with friends and was last seen when the father of one of them had dropped him outside his house. His parents only noticed he had not returned home after they went to wake him up next morning. At first they were not unduly worried. Their son had a large group of friends, several of whom they knew well, and they often stayed over at each other's houses. But when he had not returned by lunchtime they had started ringing around and soon found out that he had been dropped off outside their house the night before. They immediately rang the police. In spite of a large search of the area and an even bigger poster campaign no one had seen or heard from him. His friends were interviewed and all told the same story: he was a nice guy who didn't have any enemies. They'd had a few farewell drinks in the pub because he was going to university the next day and that was the last time any of them had seen him. They'd all known each other since primary school, played for the same football team and chased the same girls. He was just a regular kind of guy. The car of the parent who had given him a lift was searched but nothing suspicious had been found. His own parents were interviewed at length and the house searched but to no avail. When an appeal on *Crimewatch* attracted no new leads the case was left open but no longer actively pursued. The poor parents' lives were shattered and in fact both of them died before their time.

Eva found herself getting quite emotional. What an ordeal it must have been for the parents, with so many questions left unanswered. They must have asked themselves why and where a thousand times over. She shook her head to concentrate on the task in hand. Could he be the person they were looking for? Not impossible, but not very likely she decided. There seemed to be no link, either to the airfield or to an interest in environmental issues. She made another coffee and opened the next file. This one was rather thin and concerned a young man called William Gunn. She scanned the introduction and suddenly found herself getting excited. Apparently Mr Gunn had been reported missing by a friend of his, Richard Evans. What was really interesting was that both men were part of the protest against the nuclear waste dump. She read on and decided to give Steve a call.

Steve had just arrived back when his phone rang. Before he had a chance to speak he heard Eva's excited voice.

'Steve, I think I may have found our missing person.'

'That's quick,' Steve replied. 'What makes you so certain?'

'Listen to this,' she said. 'Twenty-seven year old male, one of the activists in 1996. Reported missing by someone called Richard Evans, one of the other people at the protest. Police found his bike locked up at Downham Market Railway Station but there was no sign of him. They interviewed some of the station staff but no one remembered seeing him getting on or off a train. As the bike was still there it was presumed he had taken a train, possibly to London. That was what his friends thought anyway. They recalled him leaving the protest every three weeks for a few days and knew he had been working in London. But no one knew his address. The police visited his parents but they hadn't heard from him for more than three years. Apparently they'd had a falling out over politics and he'd left the house, never to return. "Probably shacked up with some hippie in a commune," his father had remarked. Soon after this planning permission for the nuclear waste site was refused and the protesters left the area. It seems that with no one pushing for him to be found the police soon gave up looking.'

'Good work,' Steve said admiringly. 'That sounds really encouraging. Have you got many more files to go through?'

'Just one but I've already had a quick look and it doesn't appear very promising.'

'Okay, photocopy everything you think is relevant and I'll see you back at the station later on. By the way, what was the name of this person?'

'*Bingo!*' he said to himself after he'd put down the phone. They might be wrong, of course, but something told him they were on the right track. He got in his car and decided to pay Mr Evans a visit.

Chapter 13

At around four that afternoon the whole team met back in the main incident room. Steve filled everyone in on what they had found out so far. DI Woods had not had a lot of luck with his research into the protests of 1996 but with what Eva had discovered, coupled with Steve's information from the scrapbooks, they all felt they were making progress. Steve told the others about his visit to Mr Evans. When he'd arrived the older Mr Evans had got into a panic thinking he was going to be arrested again.

'It was quite funny,' Steve said. 'A few days ago he was telling us to get rid of his son but this afternoon he was calling him to get rid of me. Anyway, Richard, his son, is quite an interesting character. He has spent most of his life working on environmental projects or taking part in direct action. That's how he came to be at the protest against the proposed nuclear dump and apparently, he's back there now, taking part in the action against the New Town development. He says he didn't know William Gunn very well but that he had respected him very much as he seems to have been a bit of an expert on nuclear waste, something borne out in the article I read. Apparently he was a very placid man who, although he took part in demonstrations, always argued against any type of confrontation. Anyway, he has no idea why he suddenly disappeared but he did remember a rumour that Mr Gunn had struck up a relationship with a local girl.'

'So what next?' asked DCS Sutton.

'I've asked Eva to visit Mr Gunn's parents. Apparently they now live in Bedford so that's not a million miles away. I know it's a long shot but you never know. If they have kept any of his belongings we might get a DNA sample which would help greatly with the identification of the body.'

When the meeting had finished Steve hurried home, had a quick shower and made his way to *The Crown* in the centre of town where he had arranged to meet Anne Trevelyan. He was slightly nervous. When walking through town earlier in the day he had noticed a poster advertising a folk evening. Apparently it was going to take place in the local bookshop. On a whim he had rung Anne who'd agreed to join him. When he suggested he would pick her up she declined.

'No way, that would mean you would have to drive the same stretch of road four times.'

Anne was waiting for him at a table outside. He leant over to give her a quick hug and peck on the cheek. They had a drink and crossed the Market Place to the High Street where the bookshop was situated. Steve had often walked past the place but had never been inside.

'Wow,' said Anne, 'isn't this beautiful?'

And it was. The bookshop was decorated with many interesting artefacts and odds and ends. An old typewriter sat proudly on top of a bookcase, a massive kite, made out of linen and bamboo, was hanging from the ceiling above the children's section and all around were bookcases jammed full of interesting titles. They paid their entrance fee and made their way to the back where a number of chairs had been set up and a small stage had been created. Before long the place was full and they were introduced to the first performer. Apparently, two local musicians were supporting the main act who would appear in the second half. Everybody was encouraged to buy raffle tickets and guess what, first prize, three books, second prize, two books, and third prize, one book.

When the first singer made his way to the stage

Steve wondered what Anne would make of it all. Was it a bad idea to bring her here? What if she didn't like folk music? He looked at her but she seemed fine, listening intently to the middle-aged man on stage who, in a broad Scottish accent, told the audience that he had recently moved to Downham Market.

'It's not all been plain sailing,' he explained. 'Me and the wife came here to retire and enjoy the countryside. One of the attractions of moving to Norfolk was the idea of going on long walks along the beach. So the missus and I set off last weekend to do just that and drove to Wells next the Sea. Well, I don't know if you've ever been there but I can assure you it's nowhere near the sea.'

The audience all laughed and he started singing one of his own songs, *Wells, Nowhere Near The Sea*. Most people obviously knew it because they all sang along with the chorus. Next he explained how his father had been a strong trade unionist and how he had similar beliefs. *It's Hard To Be A Socialist In Norfolk* was greeted with cheers and enthusiastic applause. The second act was equally entertaining and before long it was time for the interval. Anne and Steve stepped outside as it had become rather hot in the confined space of the shop.

'What do you think?' he asked Anne.

'I love it,' she replied. 'It's amazing how talented some people are, don't you think? Do you often come here?'

'I'm afraid this was the first time,' Steve confessed, before adding, 'and I was rather nervous because I didn't know what to expect or whether you'd like this sort of thing.'

'Don't worry, like I said, I'm loving it. How often do they have these evenings?'

'I'm not sure but I'll find out.'

'Well,' she said, 'do get me a ticket for the next one.'

'It's a date,' said Steve.

By eleven-thirty Steve was sitting in his favourite chair drinking a glass of Bushmills. Anne and he had continued talking about music and he was pleasantly surprised to find out that they had many of the same albums. He was listening to one now, Fairport Convention's *What We Did On Our Holidays*.

It had been a great evening. The main act had been brilliant and the evening seemed to have come to a close far too quickly. He had walked Anne to her car and they had agreed to meet up again soon.

So why did he feel uneasy? He's not sure but something, somewhere, was bothering him. His thoughts turned to Eva. Was she the problem? He was interrupted by a ping on his phone. It was Anne.

'I'm home safely, thank you for a great evening.'

'Thank you for coming,' he replied. 'It was great to see you.'

But what about Eva? Why did he not agree to meet this weekend, something they had done countless times before? Was it because of Anne? Don't be stupid, he told himself. He'd really only just met Anne and his friendship with Eva had been a constant these last couple of years. Or had he been fooling himself? Was it just friendship? Or had he secretly hoped for more? He poured himself another whiskey but couldn't settle. Even listening to Tom Waits didn't relax him so he took himself to bed where he fell into an uncomfortable, whiskey-induced sleep.

Chapter 14

Eva had set off early from her house in Downham Market. Google maps had told her that it was about an hour and a half to get to Bedford but she was not taking any chances. She'd rung ahead and Mr and Mrs Gunn were expecting her at ten-thirty. By leaving an hour early she'd make sure that she was on time. Mr Gunn had been less than welcoming when she had explained she wished to make some enquiries about their son.

'What do you want to know about that waster? We haven't seen him for nearly thirty years.'

Eva felt slightly anxious. And not just because of her imminent meeting but also because she was still a little taken aback by Steve's reaction when, after last night's meeting, she had suggested that they might go to Welney Wetland Centre over the weekend.

'I'm not sure,' he'd said, 'things might come up, I'll let you know.'

He'd never reacted like that before. Normally when either of them suggested getting together, the other would simply say, 'Yes, good idea,' or 'No, I can't,' with no further explanation necessary. *Cagey*, that's the word she would use to describe his reaction, but why? Is it because they now worked together and he thinks they should keep a distance between them? Surely, if that was the case he would have told her. Anyway, she decided, worrying about it doesn't help anyone. If she still felt like this tomorrow she would simply ask him. By the time she got onto the A428 at Cambridge she'd forgotten all about it, listening at full volume to Greg James on Radio One instead.

She arrived in Bedford exactly an hour early. She decided to drive past the house where the Gunns lived and discovered their road was just off a small row of shops, one of which looked like a promising café with a few tables and chairs outside. She parked her car, walked over to the shop and ordered a flat white and a croissant. She decided to sit outside and, although the terrace was in the shade, she enjoyed feeling the warm air of what promised to be another glorious summer's day. Before long she realised it was time to go and face Mr and Mrs Gunn. She rang the bell. The door was opened almost immediately by an elderly man who she presumed must be Mr Gunn senior.

'Come in,' he said, not totally unfriendly. 'We've

been expecting you. She's here,' he called to his wife. 'Put the kettle on love.'

Before long they were seated in the living room, Eva on a single chair and the old couple next to each other, on the settee. Eva sipped her coffee. After the excellent flat white at the café she felt like she was drinking dishwater.

Stop it, she told herself, *don't become a coffee snob.* Her thoughts were interrupted by Mr Gunn.

'Well,' he said, 'you've come all this way, what do you want to know?'

'It is possible that I might have some bad news,' Eva began. 'We have found a body and we believe it might be that of your son.'

'Oh no,' Mrs Gunn said, 'has he had an accident?'

'I'm sorry,' Eva replied, 'but the person we found didn't die recently. In fact it was most likely around twenty-five years ago.'

'I don't understand,' Mr Gunn said.

Eva explained what had been happening. She stressed that of course it might not be their son but that circumstantial evidence suggested it could be.

If Mr Gunn was shocked he didn't show it.

'I wouldn't be surprised if it was him. We warned him about hanging around with all those low-life hippies. We told him it would come to no good.' Turning to his wife he pleaded, 'didn't we love? And did he listen? No, of course not.'

'Please,' said Mrs Gunn, 'stop it. He's still our baby.' Addressing Eva she asked, 'but why have you come to see us if you're not sure it's our William?'

'It's difficult for us to be certain so we wondered if you had kept anything belonging to your son which might have traces of his DNA on it.'

'We've got nothing,' replied Mr Gunn. 'We kept his stuff in the attic for nearly fifteen years. But when I retired and we moved to Bedford I decided to get rid of it. We burnt all his clothes and gave his records and CDs to a charity shop. To be quite honest, there wasn't much else.'

His voice, Eva realised, was still carrying a lot of anger but she also detected a hint of regret and sadness.

'I'm sorry,' she said, 'I knew it was a long shot. But if we could get a sample of your DNA that would be helpful too.'

They nodded and Eva produced the test kit. When they were finished she got up to leave.

'I will keep you informed if and when we have been able to identify the remains,' she promised. 'I'm so sorry to have troubled you,' she said as she walked to the door. 'It's okay, I'll let myself out.'

She made her way back to the little car park near the shops thinking about how much she hated this part of her job. Just when she was about to open her car door she felt a gentle tug on her arm. It was Mrs Gunn.

'I'm sorry,' she said, 'I didn't think earlier on. But do you think this could be helpful?'

She handed Eva a small locket which, when she opened it, contained a lock of hair and a couple of baby teeth.

'Thank you,' said Eva, 'this will be really useful. I'll make sure you get it back as soon as we've finished with it.'

'Please forgive my husband,' said Mrs Gunn. 'He puts on this hard face but I know he's hurting inside just like me. We had such dreams ….' She was quiet for a few moments.

'In a way I hope the body you found is his. It will give us some kind of closure before we die. And if he was murdered, as you say might be the case, I hope you find whoever did this and put him away for a long time.' She started to cry. 'William was a lovely boy.' And with that she abruptly turned around and left.

Eva got in her car and made her way back to Downham Market. She drove in silence. So many broken dreams, so much misery. By the time she reached Cambridge she found herself wiping away a tear.

Chapter 15

The following morning the team had reassembled at the station. Eva related details of her visit to Bedford and explained that she had dropped the locket off at Cambridge Police Station where DS Ledbetter had promised to get a DNA comparison done as soon as possible.

'But,' she had warned, 'as this is an historic case, it might take a bit longer.'

Irritating, Steve thought, but not unreasonable. He was pleasantly surprised however when he received a phone call only a few hours later from DS Ledbetter.

'It's a match,' she informed Steve. 'There is no doubt our victim is William Gunn. I will forward the lab findings to you. I have spoken to my boss who's going to ring your DCS and suggest that your unit formally take over the investigation from now on.'

Just as he put the phone down DCS Sutton came into his office.

'I presume you've heard,' she said.

'I have,' replied Steve. 'I suggest we have another meeting. We've got a murder to solve.'
But before he called the others he rang DS Ledbetter back.

'I just wanted to thank you for your cooperation. It's good working together. Can I ask one more favour? Now that forensics have finished combing the place where the body was found and we know his identity, I suppose we should lift the restrictions on the site.'

'I agree,' the DS replied. 'I have Bob Bradley's number. I'll tell him they can start work again.'

An hour later the team were all back together. Maddie had cleared a wall and put up a number of pieces of evidence, ranging from pictures of the crime scene to some of the newspaper articles Steve found in Alan Phelan's scrapbooks. In the centre was a large photograph of William Gunn himself. DI Woods had discovered it while trawling through the internet trying to find out about the 1996 protest. Steve pointed at the picture of a tall, good-looking man with slightly unruly hair and a studious kind of face.

'I can see his father in him,' Eva said.

'That reminds me,' Steve replied, 'have you been in touch?'

'I have and I've promised them I will let them know as soon as the body can be released. I know it may sound strange but I have the feeling they are quite relieved that they finally know what happened to their son. They actually wished us luck in finding his murderer.'

'We might well need some luck. Right, let's get on with it. We need to find the current addresses of as many of the protesters as we can and start interviewing them. Sergeant Newman, could you get on with that? I suggest you start with the names underneath the photo in the newspaper. DI Woods and DC Lappinska, I want you to go through Alan Phelan's scrapbooks and familiarise yourself with all the events that were happening at the time. Then, I want both of you to go to Black Fen Drove and start door-to-door enquiries. It's a long shot but someone might just remember something. Also, Mr Gunn's name will be released to the press later on today. That in itself might trigger some memories. I myself will visit Mr Evans. I'll see you all back here at five o'clock this afternoon.

While the detectives were getting on with the case Anthony Fisher and Bob Bradley were enjoying a glass of wine on the terrace at the golf club. They had finished a late lunch and were in a good mood.

Bradley had just heard that the police cordon had been removed and that work could continue, starting the next day.

'I tell you what,' he said, 'I'll be there myself tomorrow morning at seven o'clock. Call me a poet but I just love the sound of heavy machinery getting on with the job. It's like music to my ears. First thing we'll do is fill in all the inspection holes before some other poor sod falls into one. I understand your guys have all the data they need?'

'They do indeed,' said Councillor Fisher. He had explained earlier what happened the night before and that they were now assured of a majority on the planning committee.

'There is one thing though,' he continued, 'one of the guys asked why almost all of the inspection digs were carried out near the perimeter fence.'

'Simple,' replied Bradley, 'that's where most of the building will take place. We could hardly start digging holes in the middle of the golf course could we now? Also, don't forget we still have the survey from the previous proposal in the nineties. Even though it's twenty-five years old some of the info is still relevant and valid today.'

'That explains it.'

With that both men raised their glasses and toasted what they had no doubt would be a happy and prosperous future.

When Steve arrived at the Evans' house, he was greeted in the front garden by Mr Evans senior.

'What do you want now?' he asked. 'You lot coming around here all the time is giving us a bad reputation. And you can tell your so-called undercover officer to move himself,' he said, pointing at a car parked a little further up the road.

'What do you mean?' Steve asked.

At that moment the car in question started moving but before Steve could see who was inside it suddenly did a U-turn and sped away.

He addressed Mr Evans,

'We have no one watching you or working undercover here.'

'I thought you'd say that but I don't believe it. There's been different cars parked there for the last two days. One is black, the other grey. I've written down the numbers. I told Richard about it but he said I was getting paranoid. But I've noticed he's started using the back door and leaves by way of the lane at the bottom of the garden. I'm sure he's trying to avoid being seen.'

The old man suddenly started to sound concerned.

'I just wish he would stop getting himself involved in all these protests. One day he's going to get hurt.'

This is very strange, Steve thought but he doesn't say so.

'Is Richard in?' he asked.

'At work at the advice centre.'

Steve said goodbye and returned to his car. He rang the station and asked Maddie to run a couple of number plates through the system. She did so while he held on. It appeared they both belonged to the same company in Peterborough.

'What kind of company?' he asked.

'It's a private detective agency,' she replied. 'Wait a minute, I'm on their website. They are called Posh Security and offer discreet surveillance as well as security staff for shops and nightclubs, that sort of thing.'

'Thank you,' said Steve, 'that's helpful,' even though for the moment he had no idea what to do with the information he had just been given.

When he got to the advice centre he was just too late. Apparently Mr Evans had received a phone call, after which he had left early saying he needed to go to an urgent meeting. *I'm not making much progress*, Steve thought to himself, before he decided to try Alan Phelan's office. Here he was in luck. Alan was free and happy to talk to him.

'Have you come to return my scrapbooks?' he asked.

'Not yet,' said Steve, 'if it's alright we'd like to keep them a bit longer. He explained what had happened and that they now knew the victim was William Gunn and that the detailed pathology report stated unequivocally that the cause of death was a violent blow to the head. Murder therefore.

'How sad,' said Alan, 'I remember him. He was a quiet man but when he spoke they all listened. I recall interviewing him and being impressed that someone like him with a good job would give it all up to fight for his convictions.'

'I know,' Steve replied, 'I read your article.'

'So how can I help?' asked Alan.

'I'd like you to tell me anything you remember of that time. Names would be good but also, I need to get a general feel for who these people were, and where the dividing lines might have caused conflict, that sort of thing.'

'No problem,' said Alan, 'I'm not sure if I'll be much use but as I said I remember that time well because it was really my first proper assignment as a journalist. But if it's all the same with you, could we do it at your office a bit later on? I think it might be helpful if I had my scrapbooks at hand to jog my memory.'

'Great idea, thank you,' said Steve. 'Shall we say around four o'clock?'

While he was walking back to his car his phone rang. It was Anne.

'Sorry to ring you at work,' she said, 'but I need to talk to you. Can I come and see you?'

'Of course,' said Steve, 'is something the matter? You sound upset.'

'I'd rather not say over the phone if you don't mind.'

'No worries,' said Steve, 'I have arranged to meet my dad for supper at seven o'clock in Ely. Would it be too late if I pop in at yours around eight-thirty?'

'That would be great,' replied Anne.

Chapter 16

Richard Evans was confused and not sure what to do. After leaving the office he had made his way back to Downham Market. He was trying to gather his thoughts. There was no doubt that he was being followed. But why? And now this phone call. The man on the end of the line had introduced himself as an accountant working for the person who had recently made him a generous donation. Could they meet?

Richard had agreed, mainly out of curiosity but he also had the feeling that it was not so much a request, more of a demand. *Had he been really stupid?* He realised he should never have accepted the money. He should have gone straight to the police. That Detective Culverhouse seemed to be a likeable person. He would have known what to do. But instead he rang Alan Phelan's office only to be told that Mr Phelan was in a meeting. He looked at his watch. He had agreed to meet the accountant outside Greggs in ten minutes. He started walking towards the town centre and stopped when he reached the car park adjacent to the café and bakery. A man was standing next to a car parked right outside. He recognised the model. It was the same car he had seen outside his house. He felt uneasy and decided to turn around and give Inspector Culverhouse a ring. But when he did so he bumped straight into another man. He felt something hard pressed against his side.

'Keep walking to the car,' the man told him. 'Don't do anything stupid. I've got a gun.'

Richard felt as if he was in a bad dream. All around him people were going about their normal business and no one seemed to notice the two men walking close together to a car where a third person opened the back door and greeted him.

'So glad you could join us, get in.'

Richard did as he was told and was followed in by the man with the gun. The driver got behind the steering wheel and within minutes they left town and were on their way.

After Alan Phelan had left his office Steve made his way to the incident room. There he met DCS Sutton who was scanning the admittedly meagre evidence on the wall. She turned to face Steve.

'What do you think?' she asked him.

'I'm just glad it's an historical case,' he replied.

'What do you mean?'

'So far we have very little to go on. If this was a recent murder I'd be worried about the lack of progress. After all there would be a murderer on the loose.'

'Who's to say the murderer doesn't still live around here,' DS Wood suggested.

He had entered the room without either of them noticing.

'Fair point,' said Steve, 'but we've checked, and there was only one other unsolved murder in the area over the last twenty-five years and that one, being part of a sexual attack, suggests a whole different profile. No I'm sure,' he continued, 'Mr Gunn's killing is somehow linked to those protests against the proposed nuclear waste dump.'

By now Eva and Sergeant Newman had also joined them.

'Okay,' said Steve, 'what have we found out?'

DI Woods looked at Eva,

'Shall I start?' She nodded.

'We've probably covered three quarters of the houses in the village. Everyone was keen to talk about the fact that someone was murdered nearby but we soon found out that quite a few people had only moved there within the last twenty-five years. A lot of them hadn't even heard about the protests. Most of these people seem to work in Cambridge

and I suppose that's why so many weren't in.'
Steve nodded, he had often heard his father complain that the village had been taken over by newcomers. It reminded him of a song he heard at the folk club the other night;

> *And the old folks wonder*
> *Why the young ones moved away*
> *Well, the answer's simple*
> *They could not afford to stay*

It was true, many young people couldn't afford the house prices in the village so any property becoming vacant was soon snapped up by commuters from Cambridge.
While he was lost in thought DI Woods continued.

'To be quite honest, the whole thing was a bit of a waste of time. The few people left who were living in the village at the time were keen to point out that they had nothing to do with the protest even though almost everyone said they were all anti the idea of having a nuclear dump next door. But we did come across one interesting person, Eva, you met her. Why don't you continue?'

'Thanks,' said Eva, 'yes, I knocked on this door and heard a man and woman arguing, or maybe not arguing as such but definitely discussing something quite loudly. When I rang the bell a woman in her forties opened the door. She looked a bit flustered. When I told her who I was and why I was there she said she'd be happy to talk but that she was busy right now. Then she said, "I'm a friend of your boss, I'll talk to him."'

With that she turned towards Steve who felt all eyes were on him,

'You must have met Anne,' he said. 'She's an old school friend and we've recently met up again.'

'Well,' laughed DI Woods, 'you'd better give her a ring. She seemed keen to talk to you.'

'I'll do that in the morning,' Steve promised. Turning to Sergeant Newman he asked,

'Dave, how did you get on locating people?'

'Not bad. I've got the contact details for nine people so far. Seven of them were protesters. One was the chair of the planning committee and the last one is Arthur Turner who owned the land at the time. The last two and four of the activists still live locally.'

'Great,' Steve said. 'If you, DI Woods and DC Lappinska could have a closer look and divide them between you we can start contacting them tomorrow. But before you do, let's have a quick meeting in the morning and come up with a list of questions we can all refer to. Oh, and leave Arthur Turner to me. He's someone I'd like to interview myself.'

'How did you get on with Alan Phelan?' DCS Sutton asked.

'Very well,' Steve replied, 'I mean I didn't learn anything new really, but I think I've got a bit more of an idea what the issues were at the time. It is clear that for some people the burying of nuclear waste was the main issue but for others like Mr Turner, who owned the site, it was more about getting angry because he couldn't get his own way and he blamed the activists for that. Oh yes, I also learnt that when the planning decision was reached, the main objection to the site was the one William Gunn had been talking about all the time; the soil structure of the fen with its layers of peat and ever shifting water table is simply not stable enough for burying any hazardous materials, let alone nuclear waste, even if it was encased in concrete. So even though Arthur Turner saw the decision as a personal attack on him by the *"left wing greenies"* as he called them, the final decision was taken on purely scientific grounds.

While Steve was driving to Ely later that evening his thoughts turned back to the meeting. When he was walking to the car park Eva had caught up with him and asked if he fancied a drink.

'I can't,' he'd replied, 'I'm meeting my dad at seven o'clock in Ely for a meal.' Why hadn't he been up front with her? Why had he said during the meeting that he would ring Anne in the morning knowing full well that he was seeing her tonight? His thoughts shifted. Not only was he seeing her, he was also very much looking forward to it, even though he was aware that Anne was obviously upset. Who was she arguing with he wondered? Probably her son. Maybe that's what she wanted to talk to him about. Yes, that'll be it. He stopped at a garage and bought a large bunch of flowers.

Chapter 17

Richard Evans was looking around his cell. It wasn't a real cell of course but as far as he was concerned it might well be. Before they left him the two men who had brought him here had asked if he wanted something to eat and drink. In spite of being extremely anxious and worried Richard realised he was actually hungry.

'Yes please,' he'd replied, 'but nothing with meat.'

'Right you are,' the younger of the two had said, 'no worries, I'm a veggie myself.'

So they had left him alone in a room somewhere in Peterborough. It was clear where they were going the moment they had passed Wisbech. The fact that they hadn't blindfolded him gave him some confidence. It somehow didn't feel like he'd been kidnapped. Who was he kidding, what about the gun? He got up and walked to the door. It was locked. He put a chair against the wall, climbed on it, and looked out the high window. All he saw were some flats not far off. He remembered they used the lift but hadn't registered how many floors up they went. What did they want? He checked for his phone but couldn't find it. Did they take it off him? He couldn't remember. He suddenly felt extremely tired but thought of something he once read,

"Don't worry if they shout or threaten you, it means you are doing something right."

He'd always thought those were fine words. But how does that help him now? All he knows is that he was scared, very scared.

Steve sat opposite his father in *The Cutter*, a smart pub and restaurant on the waterfront in Ely. They were waiting for their main course. Steve's dad looked at his son.

'What's on your mind?' he asked, 'you look tired. Are they working you too hard?'

'It's nothing,' Steve replied, 'just this case of the body at the airfield, we're not really getting anywhere with it.'

'Sorry to hear that,' his dad said, 'I'm sure you'll solve it. I remember that time well. You had just left home to join the Met and your mother and me, well let's just say I tried to be out of the house whenever I could. As you know I'm not a drinker but I have to

admit I spent a lot of time in the pub back then.'
Steve suddenly perked up.

'Do you remember anything specific from that time?'

'Not really,' his dad replied, 'but most of the locals supported the protesters. Never openly, but I recall even your mother making a big pan of soup and dropping it off at their tents. After all, none of us wanted to live next to a nuclear waste dump.'

'And now you'll be living next to a massive new development,' Steve said, 'I wonder what's worse. After all, once it was buried you wouldn't have been able to see the waste.'

'Ah, I've got some news on that,' his father replied. But just then the waiter brought them their food and for the next twenty minutes they ate in silence. When they had finished Steve reminded his dad.

'You were saying?'

'Ah yes, you know I told you the company behind the New Town offered to buy my ten acres. Well, I've had another offer.'

Steve looks surprised.

'And you know what, they've offered me £2000 per acre more than the previous offer.'

'Who are they?' Steve wanted to know.

'I don't know,' his father replied. 'But a firm in

Cambridge act as their agents.'

'What, an estate agent?'

'No, a firm of solicitors. You know the ones I mean. They've got those new offices in the business park near the station. All glass. I don't know how the place doesn't fall down.'

'So what are you going to do?'

'Nothing for the time being,' answered his dad. 'I'm going to sit back and wait. Maybe the original company will offer me even more. But whatever happens, I won't do anything without discussing it with you and your sister first. Oh, and I've made an appointment to see my own solicitor next week. No harm in getting some advice. How about a coffee before you leave?'

'Sorry dad, I can't,' and he told him about his meeting with Anne later on. His father winked at him.

'Business or leisure?'

Steve thought about that for a minute.

'To be honest dad, I don't know.'

While Steve and his dad were having dinner Richard Evans was wondering what was going to happen next. He felt a bit better after, at one point, working himself up into an emotional frenzy. What did these people want? And, if it came to it, how much is he

prepared to tell them? '*Stay calm,*' he told himself.
He thought back to a non-violent, direct action training session he had attended. "*What to do or say in case you get arrested.*" Stick to the facts he was told. Don't volunteer information but also don't deny it if they confront you with a truth. Try to engage with individual officers about the issues but never show anger or emotion about your own situation, only about the cause itself. And do question why you have been arrested and on whose authority. Okay, he was not arrested but he was being kept against his will. Just then he heard some noise outside. The door opened and the two men came in bringing with them several cups of coffee, some bottles of water and an array of sandwiches.

'You choose first,' they invited Richard.

He selected one of the sandwiches and took a cup of coffee. That felt good. He was already getting stronger, especially mentally. It was funny what a bit of caffeine can do to put some metal in your thinking.

'Why are you keeping me here?' he asked. 'What have I done to upset you? And where is my phone?'

'Eat first,' the older of the two said, 'we'll talk later.' They were silent for a few minutes.

'Sorry about earlier,' the same man said, 'I thought you had changed your mind and were going to run away. That's why I pretended to have a gun.'

'But, but…, you did have a gun.'

The man laughed and reached into his inside pocket. Richard felt totally foolish as he looked at the toy gun. It did appear quite realistic but not on closer inspection. Even though he felt stupid he was also relieved.

'What do you want from me?' he asked.

'Information,' the younger one said.

'What kind of information?'

'Let's start again,' suggested the older of the two. 'Let us ask the questions and you simply give us the answers. The sooner we finish the sooner we can all go home. Agreed?'

'Okay,' replied Richard.

'First of all, what have you been talking to the police about?'

'Nothing,' he replied, surprised by the question.

'Don't play games with us,' the younger man intervened. 'We've seen two uniformed officers go to your house followed by a visit from the Detective Chief Inspector himself.'

'Oh that, the uniformed were there because my dad had rung them saying there was an intruder in the house.'

'And was there?'

'No, but we'd had an argument and he was just

playing silly buggers.'

'So why the senior detective?'

'That was something totally different. He was interested in the body they found at the old airfield. They had a name and asked if I had known him at the time.'

'And had you?'

'Yes, like I told the detective. I did know him but not very well.'

'Did the detective ask anything else?'

'Like what?' Richard played for time.

'Did he ask about the current protest?'

'Is that why I'm here?' Richard asked. 'Because I want to protect our countryside?'

'Just answer the question.'

'No, he didn't ask about the current protest.'

'What do you know about the site, Mr Evans?'

'It's an old airfield isn't it? Our protest is not against the airfield but about the plans to build on the land around it.'

'Do you know anything about the site being contaminated?'

'What do you mean?' Richard asked quietly. The other two picked up on this.

'You've gone quiet Mr Evans. I repeat the question. Have you heard anything about the site being contaminated?'

'Contaminated with what?'

'Just answer the question will you,' the younger man said, obviously getting annoyed.

'I have no idea what you're talking about.'

'What have you done with the £10,000 you received?'

'Nothing yet,' Richard replied, 'I want to think about the best way to use it.'

'Any ideas yet?'

'Listen, if this guy, whoever he is, wants his money back, just say so and I can get it for him tomorrow.'

'Where is it now?'

'In a safety deposit box in Peterborough.'

'Do you have the key on you?'

'No I don't,' he replied, 'anyway you can't access the room until ten o'clock tomorrow. But you're welcome to meet me there.'

'I don't think that will be necessary.'

'One final question. Why did you go and see the editor of the Fenland Gazette?'

'Oh, that's simple, I wanted to get some extra publicity for our campaign.'

'Are you sure that's all?'

'I'm sure.'

'In that case I think we're done. We just have to wait until I hear from my boss.'

Both men left the room and Richard hoped they didn't hear the sigh of relief that escaped his mouth the moment they shut the door.

'You absolute morons,' the man shouted down the phone after the older of the two had rung him.

'What do you mean?' he asked fearfully.

'Even though I gave you precise instructions to let him do the talking, lean on him a bit, frighten him a bit, you've ignored all of my instructions.'

'But, but … we haven't.'

'Do you want me to list them?' the man shouted. 'Have you forgotten that I was listening in on the whole conversation?'

'No….but.'

'Shut up,' the man on the other end of the phone said. 'First of all, whose stupid idea was it to pretend you had a gun and then drive him in clear daylight to Peterborough so he will know exactly where he was kept? Giving away the address in itself will cost us lots of money. We'll now have to find somewhere new and remove all our equipment from the place before the police hear about it.' His voice got louder again.

'And then you asked him what he knew about the site being contaminated? Have you lost your mind? That's as good as giving it to him on a plate. If he didn't know he does now and his type will not let that sort of thing rest.'

'What do you want us to do?' the older man asked gingerly.

'Nothing. You've done enough damage as it is. Stay with him until I'm able to find someone else to take care of things. Wait there until you hear from me.'

When Steve arrived at Anne's house she opened the door before he had a chance to ring the bell. When he gave her the flowers she burst out crying.

'Come in,' she said through her tears. 'Coffee, tea, wine?'

'I'll have a coffee,' Steve decided, slightly overwhelmed and a little concerned by Anne's emotions.

'I'm sorry,' she said, 'you must think I'm stupid.'

'Not at all,' he reassured her, 'but please tell me what the matter is, maybe I can help.'

'I do hope so,' she said, 'because right now I'm in a mess.'

With this she disappeared into the kitchen and returned with a coffee for Steve and a white wine for herself.

'You don't mind if I have a drink do you?'

'Not at all,' said Steve, 'I'd like one myself but I

still need to drive back to Downham tonight.'

'You're not staying at your dad's then?'

'Not tonight,' he replied, 'now tell me what's bothering you so much.' She was quiet for a moment.

'I don't really know where to start, I haven't worked it all out for myself yet.'

'Why don't you start at the beginning,' Steve suggested. She smiled.

'Thanks, it might help me to order things in my head a bit. Mind you, it could take some time.'

'No problem.'

'Okay, I know you are aware of the protests here in the nineties. One of your colleagues wanted to talk to me about it this afternoon but I would rather you heard the story from me.'

Steve wondered where this was going, but he didn't say anything.

'I think you had just left for London when the first activists arrived. I didn't take much notice at the time. I had recently got engaged and was preparing to get married. With the benefit of hindsight I was far too young, only nineteen, but my parents were keen for me to tie the knot, sooner, rather than later. I realise now that they were worried I might change my mind if we had too long an engagement. They were friends with my fiancé Geoffrey's parents who were a prominent land owning family near Oundle. Geoffrey himself was five years older, public school educated and to be quite honest, a bit boring. But for me at the time it was all very exciting. I'd never had a real boyfriend before so I went along with the whole thing. Don't get me wrong, there wasn't really anything wrong with Geoffrey, it's just….' she took a deep breath, 'I don't know if you remember, but we had a couple of black labradors at the time and I had taken to going on long daily walks with them. I had planned to find a job somewhere but Geoffrey insisted that his future wife didn't need to work.' She looked at Steve.

'Unbelievable now that I went along with it but there you go.'

'Anyway, on one of my walks I found myself near the camp at the old airbase. One of the protesters came up to me and started playing with the dogs. You know what labradors are like, you give them a little bit of attention and they are all over you.' She paused and took a large swig of her wine.

'Anyway, before long I found myself visiting the camp every day. And more often than not, this guy, Billy his name was, joined me and the dogs for part of the walk.' She looked Steve straight in the eye. 'I don't mind telling you, I pretty soon fell in love with him. I'm sorry Steve, it's getting a bit embarrassing now but you have to hear this to understand my predicament today.'

'Don't worry,' Steve replied, 'I'm a policeman, I'm sure I've heard worse.'

He immediately regretted his use of words but Anne didn't seem to mind.

'This guy was so different from anyone I'd ever met before,' she continued. 'He was serious, he was funny but what really attracted me to him was that he so obviously enjoyed my company too.'

She cleared her throat.

'About a week or two before I met Billy, Geoffrey and I had sex for the first time. It was a bit awkward but I presumed that's how it was.' She refilled her glass and continued.

'But then one afternoon I'd gone to the camp without the dogs. Billy and I went for a long walk together. And then we made love.' She blushed.

'It made me realise how amazing sex could be. All I wanted after that was to be with Billy. I was planning to break my engagement as soon as possible. I told my parents that I had doubts about marrying Geoffrey but they just said that was normal, and that all girls felt like that before their wedding day. I remember my father saying, "I think the sooner you marry the better it is for all of us."'

She hesitated.

'Not long after, I found out I was pregnant. I was totally confused so I went to see Billy at the camp to ask him what he thought I should do. We had a chat but were interrupted. We promised to meet again the next day. Just when I was saying goodbye to him my father drove past. He stopped the car and told me to get in. He was furious. He wanted to know who it was I was talking to, how I knew him and told me in no uncertain terms that I was not allowed to set foot anywhere near those dirty hippies again. So I broke my promise to Billy and didn't go the next day. I've always regretted that.'

'But,' Steve can't help interrupting, 'now your dad has joined a similar protest himself.'

'I know,' Anne replied, 'ironic isn't it? Anyway when we got home I lied and told them that the guy I'd been talking to was a friend I knew from sixth form. That seemed to calm my dad down a bit.' She looked at the clock, it was nearly eleven.

'I'll make it quick,' she said. 'I got married and gave birth to our baby seven months later. But as you already know, the marriage didn't last and Geoffrey and I went our separate ways. My parents were disappointed but I'm sure they were expecting it deep inside. At least they never held it against me. Geoffrey has been a good father to Paul, seeing him regularly and supporting him financially through school and university.'

'What about Billy? Did you ever see him again?' Steve asked.

'Well that's just it. Not long before I got married I went back to the camp to say goodbye and to explain what had happened. But he wasn't there. One of the others told me that he had left one day, never to return. I was disappointed but not really surprised. Now of course I know why and I feel terrible.'

'Well,' said Steve, 'that's quite some story. And then you became a teacher and now, here you are, you've done well for yourself.'

'Thanks,' replied Anne, 'for years I thought the same, but now it has all come back to haunt me.'

Steve waited for her to continue.

'It's so embarrassing and stupid and it has caused so much hurt but I have to tell you….. Well, now you've identified that body, today I tried to talk to Paul about Billy and it all got a bit out of hand and…..

Before she finished her sentence, the door opened and her son walked into the room.

'It's alright mum,' he said, putting his hand on her shoulder. 'It's all gonna be alright.' He turned to Steve and introduced himself.

'Mr Culverhouse, I'm Paul, Anne's son.'

Before him stood a tall, good-looking young man with a rather studious face. In fact the spitting image of William Gunn.

Chapter 18

When Steve arrived home it was way past midnight. His head was spinning and he should have gone to bed but instead he poured himself a glass of Bushmills and sat down in his favourite chair. But he didn't put any music on. He needed to think.

Anne's story had thrown up a lot of new information and might well mean they had to look at William Gunn's death from a totally different angle. Could his murder really be the result of a love triangle? Unlikely, thought Steve, but there was no doubt it was a line of inquiry they had to follow up. In his head he was already starting to compile a list of people they would need to interview, starting with her ex-husband. He suddenly realised that the list must include Anne herself. That being the case he would no longer be able to meet her as a friend. Sarah Sutton would insist he hands the case over to someone who was less close to a possible suspect. He laughed. Anne potentially guilty of murder? No way! But the thought made him feel uneasy. He hoped Anne would understand that while the investigation was going on he wouldn't be able to see her. He poured himself another whiskey. He recalled Anne's last words while they were saying goodbye on her doorstep. She'd thanked him and told him how happy it made her that they had bumped into each other again. He'd kissed her on the cheek. She had put her hand on his arm and said, "Look after yourself and drive carefully."

Not bad advice as it turned out because just when he came to the junction near the airfield, a van had passed him at great speed, almost forcing him off the road. It happened very quickly but he had just been able to recognise the logo: Mick Mendham Agricultural Services. Just before he fell asleep in his chair he told himself to ring Mick tomorrow and ask him to remind his drivers not to use the road as a race track.

While Steve was talking to Anne, Richard Evans was getting more and more concerned. A couple of hours previously he had the feeling his ordeal was nearly over but then the two men had returned and told him that they would have to wait until their boss had made up his mind on what to do next.

That was at least four hours ago. He had no idea what had happened but the two men were now refusing to speak to him and were obviously uncomfortable themselves. Finally he heard the sound of someone approaching the door. It opened and in stepped a heavily built, middle aged man.

'You can go,' he told the two men. 'Make your way back to town. You'll get a call at some point telling you what to do next.' He turned to Richard.

'You,' he said. 'The boss wasn't very impressed with your answers earlier on so we are going to try again. And take my advice, no bullshit this time. If you wanna get out of here in one piece, I suggest you answer and answer quickly.' He got out a phone and dialled a number.

'I've got him here, he's ready to talk.'

He turned the sound to speaker phone and placed the mobile in front of Richard.

A voice he didn't recognise spoke.

'Mr Evans, we haven't met. And I can assure you that it's much better for you if we never do. I don't like your type. I don't like what you stand for and I definitely do not want you or your cronies meddling in my business. So I'm going to ask you a few simple questions. What happens to you after that will depend on your answers. Are you ready?'

Richard didn't know what to think. Again he felt he was caught up in some nightmare film scenario.

'I get it,' he said.

'Okay then. What do you know about any contamination issues relating to the old airfield?'

'I've heard rumours that someone has been dumping waste illegally there over the years.'

'And do you have any proof?'

'No, I don't.'

'Do you have any documentation relating to this possible illegal waste dumping? You know the sort of thing I mean, photographs, invoices etc.'

'No I don't.'

'Let's, for the sake of argument, presume you are lying, what would publicising that evidence mean?'

'It would trigger a new enquiry into the suitability of the site as the right place for a new town.'

'Anything else?'

'I suppose, whoever dumped the waste illegally could be prosecuted if they ever found out who it was. But that is very unlikely; anyway he'd probably get away with a fine. Very few cases of illegal dumping are actually followed up unless …'

He paused.

'Unless what?'

'Unless the material dumped constituted a serious health risk.'

'Thank you, next question,'

'What did you talk to the editor of the Fenland Gazette about?'

'I've already told the other two. I wanted to get more publicity for our protest against the new town.'

'Yes, you said. Do you care to add a bit more detail?'

'Sorry, I don't know what you want me to say. I've told the other two everything I know. You have to let me go. Don't worry, I won't say anything about today to anybody.'

He was pleading now and almost close to tears.

'Please, I need to get home. My dad is old, he'll be worried and he needs me.'

'Just one more question. Have you told me everything you know? Think carefully before you answer.'

Richard contemplated the question before answering.

'I have.'

'Okay, the money you received. I'd like it back.'

'Like I told your colleagues, I can get it tomorrow at ten o'clock.'

'Or you could give us the key to the safety deposit box just so we're sure you're not going to change your mind.'

'Like I told the others, I don't have it on me, it's at home.'

Addressing the other man in the room the voice on the phone continued.

'Turn off the speaker phone.'

Richard watched as the other man listened intently, holding the phone closely against his ear.

'No worries, will do,' he heard him say, 'I'll see you there later.'

He put the phone away. Richard was just about to ask what was happening when the man told him to empty all his pockets inside out and to put all his belongings on the table. Richard did as he was told.

'So you really don't have the key to the deposit box. Shame really.' Richard wanted to ask why but he was too tired.

'Can I go home please,' he whispered.

'Of course.' the man said. 'Get yourself ready.'

Chapter 19

In spite of having only a few hours' sleep Steve felt remarkably awake. Rather than having breakfast at home he stopped at a new café in town he'd been meaning to visit. He ordered a cappuccino and a croissant before looking around for a table.

'Join me if you like.'

Eva was seated a few tables back from the counter and Steve made his way over.

'Great minds think alike, how are you?'

'I'm good,' she replied. 'Isn't this lovely?'

Steve was a little confused.

'What, meeting me here?'

'No, I mean the café.'

Now he felt embarrassed. What was it with him he thought? Eva's a friend, that's all, so why did he care so much how he came across to her.

'Don't get me wrong,' she continued, 'it's good to see you. We haven't really seen that much of one another. You seem a bit preoccupied of late.'

Just as Steve was about to answer, his coffee and croissant arrived and they heard a familiar voice.

'So this is where my officers spend their time?' said Chief Superintendent Sarah Sutton.

'Mind if I join you?'

They moved over to a larger table at the back of the café. 'Isn't it great here?' Sarah continued. 'Good coffee and I love the décor.'

They agreed.

'I have some news,' Steve told the other two.

'Is it to do with the case?' Sarah asked.

Steve nodded.

'Let's wait until we're at the station and enjoy our coffee in peace,' she said.

While the three detectives were sharing a morning coffee, Bob Bradley was standing at the entrance gate to the old airfield. He was in a good mood. The weather looked promising, there was no sign of protesters anywhere and a number of vans and minibuses were arriving bringing in the workforce to continue with the initial site preparation. It was a bit of a risk doing this before the official planning application had been approved but after meeting Anthony Fisher he was no longer concerned. Surely, having ensured that the majority of committee members were on his side meant that the plans would simply be rubber stamped. Today was all about getting back to work, starting with filling in the inspection holes.

'Ah, just the man I want to see,' he heard someone say. He turned around and saw the familiar figure of Mick Mendham walking towards him.

'Good morning, what can I do for you?'

'I'm not sure,' Mick replied, 'did you get a report last night about someone breaking into the site?'

'No, I didn't,' said Bob, 'what's happened?'

'You know someone has been tampering with some of my equipment. As a result I asked the security guy to ring me directly if he saw anything suspicious. Well he contacted me last night around eleven o'clock saying he'd heard voices and then saw a car driving away from the gate on the other side. I made my way over as soon as I could and checked my equipment but it doesn't look like anything has been damaged. My guys are now doing a more detailed check, you know, brake pipes and that kind of thing.'

'I haven't heard anything,' Bob replied, 'what did the security guard say when you turned up?'

'Not much more than what he told me over the phone. He'd heard some voices and started to make his way over there, but by the time he'd arrived he saw a car leaving.'

'Could simply have been some youngsters,' suggested Bob. 'One of my guys said he found some drug paraphernalia in the lay-by near the gate a few days back.'

'I suppose it could be something like that,' Mick agreed. 'Anyway, it's good to be back on site.'

'Absolutely.'

Just then Mick's phone rang.

'Excuse me,' he said and turned away.

'You're having me on,' Bob heard him say. 'I can't believe it. That will fuck us up again.'

He put the phone in his pocket.

'Problems?' Bob enquired.

'You won't believe this,' Mick replied. 'You better come with me.'

By eight-thirty everyone working on the case had gathered in the incident room. DI Woods and Eva were looking at the list of names and addresses Sergeant Newman had compiled when DCS Sutton and Steve emerged from her room.

'Good morning,' she said, 'I know you have already made your plans for today but Steve has some information which you have to be aware of before interviewing anybody.'

Steve got up and related the main points of what he had learnt from Anne. He explained that this meant there might be a different angle to the case, something they would have to take into consideration when talking to potential witnesses.

'In addition,' he added, 'we must now also

interview Anne Trevelyan's ex-husband as well as her parents and take a formal statement from Anne herself. Because of my friendship with her, I will withdraw from this part of the investigation.'

'Who will be in charge?' Simon Woods asked.

'I will,' said DCS Sutton. 'We are short staffed as it is and it's about time I did some real policing anyway. As this is an historic case there won't be the usual time pressure so it will fit in with my other duties.'

If DI Woods was disappointed he didn't show it. At this moment Maddie came into the room.

'Sorry to interrupt you all,' she said, 'but I have just had a call from DS Ledbetter in Cambridge. They've found another body on the old airfield. She said she's on her way now and would like one of you to meet her there.'

Sarah and Steve had a quick meeting. When they returned to the room Sarah informed the others that Steve and Eva would go to the old airfield. She told DI Woods and Sergeant Newman to divide the rest of the case load between them. Before long everyone was busy getting ready.

'Let's take one of the squad cars,' Steve said. Eva was surprised, he normally preferred to take his own car so he could listen to his favourite CDs.

'You drive,' he told her. When they got in he

dialled DS Ledbetter's number.

'We're on our way,' he told her.

'I've just arrived,' she said. 'It's pandemonium here. The builders aren't happy, I've only got one uniformed with me and the whole thing is bloody weird in my opinion.'

'What do you mean,' Steve asked, 'weird?'

'Come and see for yourself,' she said, 'but make it quick please.' Steve told Eva to put on the siren and lights.

'Where on the airfield are you,' he asked.

'Haven't they told you? The body was found in the same hole where we found the other one?'

'But that suggests it happened very recently,' he said.

'Exactly,' she replied, 'and looking at the state of him he didn't enter that hole out of his own free will.'

'Are you saying......?'

'I am indeed,' she said, 'I think we've got another murder on our hands.'

As soon as their car arrived at the airfield, Steve was approached by Bob Bradley.

'Are you in charge?' he wanted to know. 'I tell you what,' he continued without waiting for an answer, 'if you're going to close the site again I am going to make a formal complaint. This is getting stupid.'

'Mr Bradley,' Steve addressed him firmly, 'you can complain all you like but before you do so, can you just tell me what has happened.'

'Simple,' said Bradley, 'we'd just started work when one of Mick Mendham's men called him to say there was a body at the bottom of the hole he was just about to fill in. The same hole as before. Would you believe it?'

They walked over to the spot where DS Ledbetter and her colleague had cordoned off the scene with blue tape. Steve and Eva ducked under it. Bradley was about to follow them when Steve told him rather sharply to stay where he was and let them do their work.

'Forensics should be here shortly,' DS Ledbetter greeted them. She stepped aside. Steve and Eva were looking at the body of a man lying face down in the soil. Steve had a feeling there was something about the man that looked familiar but couldn't quite place him.

'Has anyone checked for signs of life?'

'One of the dumper drivers did. He's a first aider.' That means he might have disturbed vital evidence Steve realised.

'Don't worry,' said DS Ledbetter, reading his mind. 'He told me he was very careful. Apparently CSI is his favourite programme.'

'Well that's something I suppose,' said Steve.
He looked around and saw two men talking to Mick Mendham. He acknowledged Mick and addressed the men,

'Are you the men that found him?'

'I am,' one of them said, 'Davy here is the first aider who checked on him.'

'Thank you,' Steve says. 'You must have had a right shock. Mick, feel free to take these guys for a cup of tea or something but I have to ask you to return straight after because we will need a full statement from both of them.'

Mick nodded and the three of them moved away.
Steve walked back to the place where the body was lying.

'I feel I know him,' he said to Eva, 'but I can't place him.'

Just then the forensics team arrived. Steve talked to them briefly while they were putting on their white overalls and protective gear.

'There's not much we can do here now,' said Steve, 'let's leave them to it.'

They turned around and were met by three more uniformed officers.

'Perfect timing,' said DS Ledbetter. 'Can you relieve your colleague and make sure no one enters the sealed off area?'

It looked like all the workmen from the site had gathered to have a look. Steve made for Bob Bradley,

'Mr Bradley, you're not going to like it but we have to clear the site and that includes yourself. But before you go I want you to compile a list of all the personnel working on this site, including their contact details.'

'That will take hours,' said Bradley, clearly annoyed. 'Several of them are sub-contractors so I will have to contact their bosses.'

'Then the sooner you start the sooner you'll finish,' replied Steve, before adding, 'I suppose, with the site closed you'll have plenty of time.'

Eva looked at him; she'd seldom heard Steve using sarcasm in his dealings with the public.

Steve caught her look.

'I'm sorry,' he said, 'I shouldn't have said that last bit but there's something about him that winds me up.'

'What now?' she asked.

'I think it's best if we have a quick chat with DS Ledbetter.'

Just then the detective walked over to them, putting her phone away.

'That was my boss,' she said. 'He's been talking to your DCS and the case is yours. I've been told you can have the three uniformed for as long as you need them.'

'Pity,' she said while unlocking her car, 'this was starting to look like an interesting case.'

Whilst all this was going on Sarah Sutton stood in front of the evidence wall and tried to take it all in. She was excited. It had been years since she had headed up an investigation directly and she enjoyed the feeling. DI Woods and Sergeant Newman were on their way to interview Mr and Mrs Trevelyan, Anne's parents. She had rung Anne herself who had agreed to come to the station later on to make a formal statement. She had decided to visit the ex-husband tomorrow together with DI Woods. Apparently he still lived in Oundle and was returning from holiday later today. Her phone rang, It was Maddie telling her that a concerned neighbour had rung in to say they were worried about an elderly man next door, a Mr Evans. Apparently they'd heard some commotion during the night but weren't too worried as Mr Evans often had loud arguments with his son. Sarah smiled and remembered the story Steve had told her.

'Anyway,' Maddie continued, 'two uniformed officers went round there and found the place turned upside down with Mr Evans lying at the bottom of the stairs. They had immediately called for an ambulance and he was now on his way to the Queen Elizabeth Hospital in King's Lynn.'

'Thanks Maddie,' said Sarah, 'one of us better have a look.' Then realising she was the only detective left at the station she corrected herself.

'Tell the officers to stay where they are. I'll be there within ten minutes.'

When she arrived at the house she quickly realised that this was more than a domestic dispute that had got out of hand.

'How is Mr Evans?' she asked the police constable who greeted her at the door.

'He looked in a bad way but was conscious as far as we could tell. We asked him what had happened but he kept saying, '*I don't know where the key is.*' Sarah looked around. All the cupboard doors in the kitchen were standing open and the contents of most of the jars were spilled out over the floor. Rice, spaghetti, dried beans, even a bag of sugar had been emptied.

'Have you been over the rest of the house?' she asked the constable.

'My colleague had a quick look to see if his son was here but we thought it best to leave everything as we found it.'

'You did right. What about his son? Any sign he was involved?'

'Difficult to say,' the constable answered, 'but he's definitely not here.'

'Thanks,' Sarah told the constable. 'I'll ring forensics and then speak to the doctor at the hospital to see how Mr Evans is getting on.'

Chapter 20

When DI Woods and Sergeant Newman arrived at the home of Mr and Mrs Trevelyan the first thing they noticed was a car coming out of the drive and heading in the opposite direction. DI Woods was aware that many people did not like having a police car parked on their drive so he stopped a few doors away from the neat bungalow on the edge of town. They walked up to the front door and Sergeant Newman rang the bell. The sound of Beethoven's *Ode to Joy* chimed through the bungalow. Simon Woods smiled, now there's a ringtone he hadn't come across before. It took a few minutes before the door opened.

'I'm sorry to have kept you waiting,' Mrs Trevelyan said, 'I'm not as mobile as I used to be. I'm waiting for a hip operation but God knows when that's going to be with waiting lists the way they are. Anyway, come in. Coffee or tea?'
They were ushered into the living room while Mrs Trevelyan busied herself in the kitchen. When she

returned with the coffee and biscuits DI Woods asked about her husband.

'Is Mr Trevelyan not here?'

'No I'm sorry, he got a call and asked me to apologise to you but he had to leave urgently for an unexpected meeting.'

'That's disappointing,' DS Woods responded.

'When will he be back?'

'He told me not till later this afternoon, maybe you would prefer to come back then?'

The two detectives looked at each other. Neither of them felt like making another two hour round trip the same day.

'I tell you what we'll do,' said DI Woods, 'we'll have a chat and if there's anything we need your husband for we might ring him later. Shall we start?' She nodded. Sergeant Newman took out his notebook.

'You know why we are here?'

'I know it has to do with the body of one of the protesters you found at the airfield. But what it has to do with us I have no idea.'

'You're right,' Simon said. 'The reason we are keen to speak to you is because of what your daughter has told us. Have you spoken to Anne?'

'We have, earlier on today. I don't know what's got into her. Saying that hippie could have been

Paul's father. I told her she's got it wrong. Paul is Geoffrey's son, no doubt about it. I told her to have a DNA test as soon as possible. That will settle the matter.'

It was clear she was getting upset. DI Woods was not surprised, it must have been a tremendous shock.

'Were you aware your daughter visited the camp at the airbase several times?'

'No I wasn't, she regularly took the dogs for a walk but I never thought about asking where she was going. She was engaged to Geoffrey and we were planning the wedding. Why are you asking about Anne, you don't think she's got anything to do with all this do you?' DI Woods didn't answer.

'Were you aware that your daughter had struck up a close friendship with one of the protesters?'

'No I wasn't. The first we heard about it was earlier today. I don't mind telling you it was a shock. We are a respectable family and to think that Anne used to visit those layabouts ….'
She paused.

'My husband drove past once and saw Anne talking to some of them. He told her not to go there anymore and as far as we were concerned, that was it. Anyway, she married not long after and they moved to Oundle. It was a shock when we heard that she and Geoffrey had separated. He was such a good man, from a well-respected family too.'

'I understand your daughter came to live with you?'

'She did, of course I was angry with her at first, throwing away a secure future like that, but she had Paul by then and he was a delight to have around. So Anne went to college and then followed in her father's footsteps and became a teacher. And Geoffrey, give him his due, stuck by Paul and helped financially whenever he or Anne needed something. That's how much of a gentleman he was.'

DI Woods smiled to himself; if either DCS Sutton or DI Starling were here now they would have had trouble keeping their mouths shut and point out that what Geoffrey did was no more than his responsibility and did not need special recognition.

'One final question,' he said, 'nothing to do with the case but just out of interest. You referred to the protesters as layabouts. Yet your husband has now joined a similar protest at the same airbase. Why the change of heart?'

'You'll have to ask him, I have no idea.'

Steve and Eva were waiting for the scene of crime officers to finish their initial investigation. One of them was in the hole itself, examining the body and the soil around it. Others were combing the ground immediately adjacent to the edge for possible evidence. One of them called out. He had found a clear imprint of a shoe. Just then Mick Mendham returned with the two other men.

'Just in time,' said Steve. 'When you found the body and checked him, from which direction did you approach the hole? Both men pointed out where they had walked.

'Similar to DC Lappinska and me,' he told the officer in charge.

'That's helpful,' he said, 'but we still need to take a photo of the soles of your shoes. I'll get one of the team to do so as soon as possible.'

Steve, Eva and the others moved away.

'Are you ready to give a statement?' Steve asked the men. They nodded and he turned to Eva,

'DC Lappinska, if you could take our first aider I'll do the other one.'

It didn't take long, both men telling more or less the same story.

'Did anyone else see the body?'

'No,' the first aider said proudly, 'I told them to stay away and not contaminate the ground.'

'You did well,' Eva told him.

'Can we go now?' Mick Mendham asked.

'As soon as they've taken photographs of your shoes. I'll be in touch later if we need more information.'

They were led by the forensic photographer to the police van where they had their shoes checked and photographed. When they were finished Steve asked the team leader when they were planning to move the body.

'That will be a while yet,' he said, 'but we are ready to turn him onto his back.'

Steve and Eva put on their protective gear and walked over to the edge, just in time to see the body gently being lifted and rolled over. Even though the face was dirty and dark there was no doubt. They were looking at the battered and bruised face of Richard Evans.

Sarah Sutton had returned to the station from Mr Evans' house. She had left one of the uniformed there to deter anyone from getting too close as a small group of people had already gathered in the street outside. Just before she left the forensic team had arrived and started their work. Sarah had spoken to the hospital staff but there was no further news on Mr Evans' condition other than that he had been put in an induced coma. She needed to speak to Steve. Just then he rang and told her that the body at the airfield was that of Richard Evans.

'We are just on our way to give his father the bad news,' he told her.

'No point at the moment,' she replied, telling him about the coma. 'I think you had better get back here quickly.' She explained what had happened at Mr Evans' house. Steve was shocked.

'Not much doubt the two incidents are related,' he said. 'Okay, we're on our way.'

As soon as she put the phone down Sarah was told by Maddie that Anne Trevelyan was waiting in the foyer. Sarah made her way downstairs.

'I'm DCS Sutton,' she welcomed Anne, 'thank you for coming in.' They made their way to one of the interview rooms.

'I've told Steve, sorry, Detective Culverhouse everything already,' said Anne.

'I know, and we are grateful, but in cases such as these we need a formal statement.'

'What do you mean, cases such as these?'

'Murder,' replied DCS Sutton.

Anne looked shocked.

'Oh my God,' she said, 'the newspaper said a body had been found but not that he had been murdered.'

'And DCI Culverhouse didn't tell you?'

'No he didn't.'

'Sorry if that's been a shock to you,' Sarah said gently before continuing,

'I understand you knew William Gunn.'

Anne's face turned white.

'Yes, I did. I called him Billy,' she said, 'my Billy. That's why he wasn't there when I went to say goodbye.'

She started crying.

'I'll get us some tea.'

Steve and DCS Sutton had been talking in her office for the last half hour.

'How was your interview with Anne?' he asked.

Sarah relayed what happened and how Anne had broken down when she was told that her lover had been murdered.

'She immediately grasped the implications,' she said.

'What do you mean?' Steve asked.

'When she left she asked me if we now considered her to be a suspect. I told her that we can't rule anything out at this stage but that it would be useful if she and her son could supply us with a DNA sample. I'm just pleased for her that it's the summer holidays.'

'Why?' Steve wondered.

'If this had happened during term time she would have had to immediately inform her chair of governors who might not have had any choice but to suspend her.'

'The thing is,' he said, 'when I was talking to her the previous evening I was doing so as a friend, in fact, it was more listening than talking on my part.'

'I realise that,' Sarah replied. 'Don't beat yourself up over it. No harm done. But we are agreed then that we have to change the focus of the whole operation in the light of these latest developments?'

'Absolutely,' agreed Steve, 'and this time we can't take it as easy as we have done with Mr Gunn's death. There is a particularly nasty murderer out there somewhere. Or should we make that murderers?'

They made their way to the incident room where they relayed what had been happening to the rest of the team. Everyone was both shocked and excited. A murder, a violent attack and a break-in, they had their hands full indeed.

'So,' Sarah concluded. 'I want to re-assign duties. Sergeant Newman, DI Woods, DCI Culverhouse and myself will concentrate on the murder of Mr Evans and the attack on his father. That leaves you DC Lappinska to get on with the William Gunn case. I have asked King's Lynn police to release PC Sheldon to assist you. I know you have worked together before and I'm sure you'll make a good team. You will be directly responsible to me.'

Steve looked at Eva but was unable to read

anything in her face. Was she daunted by the task? Or was she disappointed not to be part of the new case? He couldn't tell but made a mental note to ring her later.

'Okay, that's it. DI Woods and DC Lappinska, can you come to my office please so we can share what we have learnt from our interviews today.'

In the debrief DI Woods told Eva about his visit to Mrs Trevelyan and Sarah related her interview with Anne. When the meeting finished she asked Eva to stay behind.

'How do you feel about taking responsibility for running the case?' she asked.

'I'm not exactly sure,' Eva answered, 'don't get me wrong, I'm excited and chuffed that you've asked me but do you really think I'm up to it?'

'Of course you are, I wouldn't have asked you if I didn't think you were. Anyway, DCI Culverhouse agrees with me.'

'In that case thank you very much. I'll try not to let you down.'

As soon as Sarah had finished she joined Steve, DI Woods and Sergeant Newman in the incident room. While she was talking to Eva, Steve had some time to think about what had happened.

'The way I see it,' he said, 'from the description

DCS Sutton has given us it looks like the break-in was staged to find something in particular. Although we don't know for sure of course, nothing seems to be stolen. Mr Evans' wallet was on the kitchen table, the TV and computer were untouched. All that gives me the idea they were looking for something specific.'

Sarah cut in,

'I think you're right. The uniformed officer told me that Mr Evans had repeatedly said "I don't know where the key is."'

'That sounds interesting.' said Steve, 'but what key?'

'Anyway, it looks like they didn't find what they were looking for and one possibility is that they took Mr Evans' son, beat him up and killed him as a result, dumping his body in the hole at the airfield.'

'But why?' asks DI Woods, 'what's the airfield got to do with all this?'

'He is, sorry, was a member of the group protesting against the New Town development,' said Sergeant Newman.

'So is Mr Trevelyan,' added DI Woods.

'Wait a minute,' interrupted Steve, 'Richard Evans also belonged to the original group of protesters in the 1990s.'

'Are you suggesting both cases are linked?' asked DCS Sutton.

'I don't know, we can't rule it out. It seems too much of a coincidence.'

'So where do we go from here?' someone asked. Steve stood up.

'DI Woods, take a PC with you and start interviewing all the neighbours. Check especially if any of them have CCTV on their houses. Sergeant Newman, could you concentrate on finding out more on the membership of the Anti New Town Collective?'

He turned to DCS Sutton.

'I presume you will hold the fort here for us and Eva?' She nodded and he continued.

'I will start by going to visit Alan Phelan again. If anyone knows what's going on with these protests he's probably the one. I'm also planning to see Mick Mendham on the way back.'

Even though it was now late afternoon they all made their way to start their different tasks. But just before Steve got to his car Maddie called him back.

'Forensics have emailed us the preliminary findings from the airfield.' she said.

Sarah joined them and Maddie brought up the email. It appeared they found blood away from the hole as well as evidence of several more shoe imprints. They had already done a comparison and were been able to discount Steve, Eva and Mick Mendham's two employees. One set belonged to Mr Evans which left one imprint unaccounted for. The fact that the murderer or murderers had made no attempt to remove this evidence suggested to Steve and Sarah that they were not dealing with professionals here.

'That's something I suppose.' said Steve before returning to his car.

Eva had decided to go for a walk. She needed to clear her head. So much had happened in such a short time. She'd started less than two weeks ago and now she'd already been given the responsibility to continue investigating the murder of a young man. Admittedly, it was an old case but like Steve suggested, both cases could be linked. She felt chuffed on the one hand but was also quite anxious. What if she screwed up and missed some vital evidence. Her thoughts turned to Steve. When Sarah Sutton had asked her if she saw any problems working with him she had answered honestly that she couldn't see any. Now she was not so sure. Ever since he'd bumped into his old flame he'd become a little distant. *Stop it*, she told herself, *how do you know Anne Trevelyan was an old flame?* After all Steve had referred to her simply as an old school friend. And then again, even if he had developed feelings for Anne, she should be pleased for him.

But she knew that deep inside, whether she liked it or not, she was a little bit jealous.

She had arrived at her front door but instead of going in she decided, on the spur of the moment, to return to the station to start making a plan of action for tomorrow.

Chapter 21

While Steve was driving to the offices of the Fenland Gazette, Alan Phelan rang him.

'You must be telepathic,' Steve answered, 'I was just on my way to see you.'

'The other staff have already left, just come straight in, I'll leave the door open.'

Twenty minutes later Steve arrived and the two men made themselves comfortable in Alan's office.

'I suppose you've heard?' said Steve.

'I have,' Alan replied. 'That's a rum old going on, that is. I feel really sorry for his father, lying in hospital, and as soon as he starts getting better someone will have to tell him his son was murdered.'

'I know, it's a sad business. But why did you ring me, you must have something on your mind?'

'I do, I'm not sure if you're aware but Mr Evans came to see me a few days ago. He asked me to keep our conversation confidential but I think that under the circumstances you should know the details.'

He proceeded by telling Steve about the anonymous donation and filled in a bit more of the background to Mr Evans' life.

'I'm sure he wouldn't be everyone's cup of tea but he was a genuine sort of guy, dedicating his whole life to saving the planet.'

'And do you think that some of his actions are the reason he was murdered?'

'I wouldn't be surprised. It can't be a coincidence that he was found at the same spot as his pal Billy Gunn. Oh, I forgot to say, he also mentioned that he believed he was being followed.'

'Yes,' Steve replied, 'I was aware of that. As a matter of fact we think we know the people who followed him so they can expect a visit from us first thing tomorrow morning. Do you know what he did with the money?'

'I do,' Alan replied, 'as far as I know he put it in a safety deposit box at his bank.'

Steve drove away from Wisbech towards Mick Mendham's farm. He was grateful to Alan for the information but at this actual moment not sure how it might relate to Mr Evans' death. It would be logical to think that someone was looking for the £10,000 or maybe the donor might have wanted it back. But surely, if that was the case the easiest thing for Mr Evans would have been to simply hand it over. No, there must be more to it than that. But, like Alan, he wondered why someone, who on the face of it was not rich, would feel the need to have a safety deposit box.

He arrived at the farm just as Mick Mendham was leaving. He had a young woman sitting next to him. Both men opened their windows.

'To what do I owe the pleasure?' Mick enquired. 'Whatever it is, can we make it quick, I need to get to Downham to drop my daughter off at the train station.'

'Why don't you do that first and pop in at the police station afterwards,' Steve suggested.

'How about meeting at the pub?'

'I think,' Steve said, 'that in the circumstances the police station might be a better option.'

Forty five minutes later Steve sat opposite Mick in one of the interview rooms.

'Why do I suddenly feel as if I've done something wrong?' Mick asked Steve. 'Tell me, am I in trouble?'

'That all depends,' said Steve.

'That doesn't sound too good,' Mick replied. 'Do I need a solicitor?'

'That's up to you, as far as I'm concerned. I just want to ask you a few questions. You're not under arrest and I want to thank you for coming in at such short notice. Shall we start?' Mick nodded, clearly nervous.

'You have a number of work vans with your logo on it don't you?'

'I do, seven to be precise,' answered Mick, looking confused.

'Do your drivers take these vans home or are they left overnight in your yard?'

'They always stay in the yard,' Mick replied, especially since we've had that bout of vandalism I told you about.'

'So that was the case last night?'

'Yes,' he said.

'Thanks, where were you last night between say, ten o'clock and four o'clock this morning?'

Mick visibly relaxed.

'I was at home but got a call from the security guard at the airfield who had heard some noise. My daughter had borrowed my car so I took one of the work vans and drove to the airfield. The security guard can confirm that.'

'And do you know what time that was?'

'Not exactly,' Mick said, 'somewhere between eleven and twelve-thirty. I was back home at one o'clock, I know that because my daughter and I arrived at the same time.'

'When you were at the airfield did you notice anything suspicious?'

'No, not really. The guard and I checked our equipment. I had a bit of a look around but didn't notice anything out of the ordinary. Mind you, it was dark.'

'Do me a favour,' Steve said by way of finishing the conversation. 'If you remember anything, however small, over the next couple of days give me a ring will you.'

'I will,' Mick replied, obviously relieved.

The two men shook hands and Steve saw Mick out. He believed him. He remembered the previous case when Mick's wife had said, "Mick would never murder anyone, rough them up maybe, if they deserved it, but killing? No, not my Mick."

But why, Steve wondered, had Mr Mendham been so nervous when he first came in?

After a quick meeting with DCS Sutton, Eva decided that it was time to go home. She had made good progress and now had at least some idea what she was going to do next. She felt more confident and started walking back towards her house near the station, a fair way, but she didn't mind. Just when she turned the corner near Tesco's, a car slowed down next to her and she could hear Steve's voice through the open window.

'Can I give you a lift?' he asked.

'That would be lovely,' she replied 'but I just need to go into the shop to get myself something to eat. I didn't realise how late it was.'

'I know,' said Steve, 'I can't believe it has gone past nine o'clock. How about a quick curry?'

'I had one last night,' she replied, 'but….'

'But what?'

'I wouldn't mind a chat. What about the new restaurant on the corner near the clock. That's if they're still serving.'

'Great idea,' said Steve, 'I've wanted to try them out for a while myself but haven't had a chance.'

Eva got in his car and they drove around the one way system to the town hall car park. They crossed the road and before long entered the restaurant and were immediately struck by how good and welcoming it looked inside. It was busy but they were led to a table for two by a friendly waiter who told them they were just in time. The kitchen closed in thirty minutes.

They sat in silence for a while studying the menu. After they'd made their choice they decided they deserved a glass of wine, a Pinot Grigio for Eva and a Merlot for Steve. It had been a long day. At first neither of them spoke but finally Steve said,

'Is everything alright? You seem to have something on your mind.'

'Everything's fine,' she told him 'but ...'

She stopped. She wanted to ask him why he had been so distant but was scared to approach the subject. Instead she said,

'It's just the case. It's a big responsibility and I just hope I'm up to it. I thought joining your team would see me shadowing all of you for at least the first six months. And now it's only been ten days and here I am, having to make decisions already.'

'Really,' Steve said, 'if that's all it is don't worry. DCS Sutton would not have asked you if she didn't think you were up to the job.'

'And what do you think?'

'I totally agree with her but if it helps, would you like to run your plans past me. I'm sure you've already constructed a bit of a time line for yourself.'

'I have,' she said, 'that's why I was at the station tonight. If you don't mind, I'd love to take you through it.'

Making sure they couldn't be overheard, Eva told Steve what her plans were. He listened attentively. Just when she'd finished, their meals arrived.

'I think your approach is spot on.' said Steve before they started eating. 'The only thing I want to say is that, even though this is an historical case, please do not visit any suspects or witnesses on your own. Always make sure there's someone with you. Remember what happened last time when you went to that house on the Silt Road alone?'

Eva shuddered and thought back to the time she was imprisoned against her will and her life was threatened.

'Good advice,' she replied, 'thanks.'

And with that they both tucked into their meals that were every bit as good as people had been saying.

When Eva got home she wondered if she should have invited Steve in for a coffee. After they'd finished their meal they had sat chatting for another half hour or so before Steve offered her a lift home. She looked at the clock, eleven-thirty, time to get some sleep. She wanted to make an early start, driving to Oundle to meet Geoffrey, Anne's ex-husband. She hoped she would have time on the way back to stop off in Peterborough and try to catch Mr Trevelyan at home. While getting ready for bed her thoughts turned back to Steve. She was glad he hadn't asked her who her prime suspects were. Because if he had she would have had to tell him that Anne Trevelyan was definitely one of them. She was glad it didn't come up because it had been a really nice evening. Okay, it started a bit awkwardly but soon any distance there may have been between them had disappeared. They had talked freely, not only about the case but also about Steve's relationship with his children and his dad. She had wanted to ask about Anne but chickened out, not wanting to spoil the positive vibe. *Remember girl, she told herself, friends, good friends, that's the most it will ever be between you and Steve.* And that should be enough. But just before she fell asleep she thought how nice it would have been if he had been here with her right now.

In spite of it being late Steve had decided on a nightcap before turning in. Glass of Irish whiskey at the ready he put on one of his favourite albums, Joni Mitchell's *Blue.* He sat back in his chair to let the music wash over him, his favourite way of relaxing. But he soon realised he couldn't. What stopped him were the images of Anne and Eva fighting for space in his head. He got up, annoyed with himself. He felt stupid, like a teenager in love. But who was he in love with? And who's to say that either Eva or Anne would even give him a second look. Somewhat out of sorts he had a quick second drink before going upstairs to bed.

Chapter 22

By seven-thirty the next morning the whole team, minus Eva, were assembled in the incident room. DCS Sutton welcomed everybody and informed them that she had heard from the hospital but that there was no change in Mr Evans' condition. Apparently the consultant expected that they would keep him in a coma for at least another two days.

'So there's no chance of us interviewing him,' she concluded.

'At least we have already traced the cars that were used to observe his son,' said Steve. 'I think a visit to Posh Security as soon as possible would be a good way to start. DI Woods and Sergeant Newman, could you go as soon as possible. Here's the address. He handed Simon a piece of paper on which Maddie had written down the details of the cars as well as the address of the security firm, 116A Queensway, Peterborough.

'I recognise that address,' DI Woods said, 'but I'm not sure why.'

'Take some uniformed officers with you and as soon as you have found the two men who were parked in Mr Evans' road, arrest them, and get them over here. I have spoken to our colleagues in Peterborough so they are aware.'

Just then his mobile rang. He looked at the caller ID and signalled to the others that he had to take the call. It was Alan Phelan.

'Steve, I think you'd better get yourself over here, guess what arrived in the morning post?'

Steve drove to Wisbech as fast as the bumpy and winding road along the Well Creek allowed him to. Alan Phelan was waiting for him in his office. None of the other staff had turned up yet. In front of him on the table was a letter and next to it was a key. Steve put on his rubber gloves and picked up the piece of paper.

Dear Mr Phelan,
A number of things have happened during the last week which have made me concerned about my own safety. The discovery of Billy's body brought home to me how far some people will go to silence the truth. Also the donation of £10,000 feels to me like a not very subtle attempt to either buy my silence or

compromise me. I also believe I am being followed. You might consider me paranoid but as you are the only person who I have trusted so far, with at least part of my story, I hope you don't mind that I have enclosed the key to my safety deposit box as well as a letter of authorisation for the bank, just in case anything should happen to me. I hope that I'm wrong in which case I shall pick the key up in due course.

Yours in peace,

Richard Evans

Steve looked at the second piece of paper on the table which was the letter authorising Alan Phelan to act on Mr Evans' behalf.

'What do you think?' Alan asked.

'So he obviously knew a lot of stuff about certain individuals. Pity he didn't give us more details. Sure you don't have any further information?'

Alan looked up,

'I haven't,' he said.

'No worries, I presume you don't mind me accompanying you to see what's in that safety deposit box?'

'Why do you think I rang you?' replied Alan Phelan.

Eva had set off early, picking up PC Sheldon on the way, and had reached Oundle around the same time that Steve and Alan Phelan were making their way to Peterborough. She easily found the impressive farmhouse just outside the town on the banks of the river Nene. Geoffrey Henderson was waiting for them in the drive. He was slightly overweight and his skin had a reddish colour, especially his nose.

'Come in,' he said, 'you must be ready for a drink. Sorry about the mess, we've only just got back from the Seychelles.'

He showed them into a beautiful, spotless farmhouse kitchen where a tall woman wearing blue overalls stood ready to pour them a drink.

'Meet Claire,' Mr Henderson said. 'Longtime friend, family solicitor and, I'm proud to say, my wife for over ten years. And before you wonder, you can speak freely in front of her, she knows all about my past. As a matter of fact, she was a guest at Anne's and my wedding. But that's all a long time ago.'

Eva introduced herself and her colleague and said,

'PC Sheldon will take notes.'

'Two constables hey,' replied Mr Henderson, and glancing at his wife he continued, 'they obviously don't think I'm guilty of murdering that hippie or they would have sent a higher rank.' He turned back to Eva,

'Now what can I do for you young lady?'

Eva was getting annoyed but didn't show it. The man was blatantly attempting to intimidate her by questioning her rank and status.

'Mr Henderson, the person you referred to as a hippie had a name. He was called William Gunn, approximately twenty-seven years old when he died and had a successful career as a scientist. At the protest he was known as Billy. Did you know him?' She looked straight at him.

'I didn't know *any* of them. I obviously saw them on occasion when I drove past but I never spoke to anyone. To be quite honest, I know you are only doing your job but you are wasting your time talking to me. I used to visit Anne at her parents and stayed there occasionally. Why would I talk to them?'

'So you weren't aware of any tensions between the protesters and the authorities or even the locals?'

'Not really,' he said, 'I mean I read things in the paper sometimes and heard things from Anne's father, but I never saw anything myself.'

'What sort of things did you hear?'

'The usual, the protesters shouting at councillors, that sort of thing.'

'Were you aware that Anne had struck up a friendship with one of the activists?'

'No I wasn't.'

Eva noticed he was getting angry.

'And I tell you what, if I had known I would have told her to stop it immediately and gone over myself to give the man a good hiding.'

'Geoffrey,' his wife says.

'Okay, okay, I wouldn't have hit him,' Mr Henderson retracted, 'but I would have made it clear that he was to stop talking to my fiancé.'
He raised his voice,

'And just so you know, I didn't murder him.'

'I'm not implying you did,' Eva replied calmly. 'I'm just trying to build up a picture of how things were at the time. As I understand it, you and your then wife were married for only a few years?'

'What has that got to do with anything?'
Mr Henderson was nearly shouting now. His wife put a calming hand on his arm.

'I think,' she said, addressing Eva, 'your line of questioning seems less than appropriate. I suggest that if you don't have any more questions relating directly to the death of this poor man you'd better leave.'

'Just one more question,' Eva replied, 'we would be grateful if you could supply us with a sample of your DNA. It will only take a minute, we have the kit with us.'

Mr Henderson was close to losing his temper.

'I will not,' he shouted. 'I know what this is about, Anne's father rang me last night and you are trying to say that Paul is not my son.'

'I'm afraid your information is wrong. Whether or not Paul is your son is none of our business. Your DNA would simply help us in eliminating you from our enquiries.'

'Wow!' said PC Sheldon when they were back in the car. 'What an entitled arrogant shit he was. *"We've only just got back from the Seychelles,"'* he mimicked.

Eva laughed.

'I know,' she replied. 'He likes the sound of his own voice and thought he was so clever but this way we actually learnt more.'

'Like what?' Ben Sheldon asked.

'Well we now know that he's still in touch with Anne's parents.'

'I have to say, I was impressed with you in there,' PC Sheldon said. 'You've obviously really taken to this detective stuff.'

'Thank you,' Eva replied, 'that means a lot.'

The moment they arrived in Peterborough DI Woods remembered why the address sounded so familiar. The premises of POSH Security were based right next door to the employment agency and brothel run by Derk Pieters, better known as Curly. They had met during another case while investigating the murder of a local farmer. Although Pieters himself had not faced any charges, one of his employees had been put away for sixteen years for manslaughter.

They had come in three cars and parked deliberately right outside the front door to the security premises. The uniformed officers waited outside while the two detectives rang the bell next to an impressive panelled wooden front door. It took a bit of time but after DI Woods had leant on the buzzer for at least half a minute the door was opened by a man in his thirties. He was unshaven and looked like he'd had a rough night.

'What's the fucking hurry?' he said by way of welcome.

'Can we come in please?' Simon said, showing his badge. Without waiting for an answer he pushed the door open wide and walked in.

'Oi,' the guy shouted, 'you can't just barge in like that.'

'I can and I've just done exactly that,' DI Woods replied. 'Where's your mate?'

'What do you want?' the man asked, 'don't you need a warrant?'

'Not in cases where we're actively pursuing a

murderer,' was the reply.

'Fuck off,' the man said. 'We've not murdered anyone.'

'Ah,' Simon said, 'I noticed you used the word *we*. So I ask you again, where's your mate?'

'Upstairs asleep,' was the answer.

But they didn't have to go upstairs because at that moment another man walked into the room.

'What's all the commotion?'

'It's the coppers,' the first man said. 'They're talking about a murder.'

'Well, in that case you've come to the wrong place,' the second man said. 'We've not murdered anyone.'

'Sit down,' DI Woods ordered them. 'We just want to check some facts. We have run a check on your vehicles and we know that both cars were used in the surveillance of a Mr Evans. Both vehicles are registered to the company at this address.'

'So what?' one of the men said defiantly.

The detectives ignored his remark.

'Are you the owners of POSH Security or are you employees?'

'We work for the company,' the second man said.

'Thank you, who owns the company?'

'Charlie Engledow is the manager.'

'But who owns it?'

'I think it's the guy next door, I don't know his name but he's got a funny accent.'

DI Woods and Sergeant Newman exchanged glances.

'Derk Pieters?'

'If you say so. Anyway, what's all this about, I'm tired, I need some sleep.'

DI Woods didn't answer.

'How many people work here?' he asked.

'Apart from Charlie, it's just us two.'

'So, am I right in saying that you are the drivers of both the cars I mentioned earlier?'

'We sometimes drive them.' the second man agreed.

'Where were you the night before yesterday, say after ten o'clock?' Both men visibly relaxed.

'We were next door in the nightclub,' the first one said. 'We arrived sometime after ten and stayed until about three in the morning. You can check if you like, they've got CCTV.'

Simon decided to take a chance.

'As part of your work were you asked to monitor the movements of a Mr Evans?'

'We were,' the second man admitted. 'But that's not against the law.'

'I didn't say it was,' says DI Woods. 'Just tell me about it.'

'Boring job it was. The only interesting thing was when this younger bloke and his old man used to have a shouting match in the garden.'

'Are you aware that the house was broken into and that the younger man, Mr Richard Evans, was consequently killed? And just so you know, the older Mr Evans was beaten up but is recovering well in hospital. It won't be long before he is able to identify his attackers.'

A lie, he knew, but it seemed to have worked. Both men were now obviously panicking. They looked at each other and nodded.

'We don't know anything about a murder,' the first man said,' but we admit, we did visit the house. I'm glad the old guy is alright. But we didn't do anything to him, he just started shouting and tried to run up the stairs and turned around and then just seemed to fall down.'

DI Woods looked at Sergeant Newman.

'I think we'll continue this conversation back at the station,' he said.

Steve had rung ahead to the bank in Peterborough and when Alan Phelan and he arrived they were led straight to the manager's office. He was not happy.

'This is highly irregular,' he explained. 'Normally when our clients authorise someone else to access their boxes they inform the bank themselves.'

'I'm sure Mr Evans would have done so but I'm afraid he's dead so that's rather difficult.'

'Still,' the manager said, 'I can't just let you take away his possessions, I will need to seek further advice on this.'

'We haven't got time for that. We are in the middle of a fast developing murder hunt. I believe that the contents of Mr Evans' safety deposit box may give us vital clues to the identity of the murderer. Anyway, we don't need to take it away, just check what's in there. In your presence if you prefer.'

This seemed to satisfy the manager and the three men made their way downstairs to a strong room which housed a large number of safety deposit boxes, all set securely into the walls. The manager and Alan Phelan both used their keys after which they carried the contents to a table in the middle of the room. There was not much really: The bag with the £10,000 was by far the largest item. Other than that there was an envelope with two typed letters as well as a number of photocopies of what looked at first glance like maps of the local area. Finally there was a plastic protective cover containing a number of photographs and a second envelope.

Steve put on his gloves and started reading. The first letter referred to some of the photocopies and was basically a record of land sales around the airfield from the last five years. The second letter had a list of the photographs, marking the date they were taken, as well as a short explanation of each picture. The first thing Steve noticed was the date on some of them. The photocopies were all quite recent, but some of the pictures went back as far as 1997. It soon became clear to Steve that all this stuff needed very careful analysis which would take some time. He explained this to the other two men who had kept at a polite distance.

'I will quickly take pictures of everything,' he said, getting out his phone. But just before he did so he opened the third envelope. It was a long handwritten letter and, looking at the date, only recently added.

Dear Mr Phelan,

If you read this something will have happened to me. If you have not done so already I trust you will inform the police. All this started in 1997. A few months after planning permission was refused and all the other activists had left, I noticed a small truck entering the airbase while I was cycling past. I thought nothing of it but then a few weeks later I saw the same truck again. I started wondering what it was doing there. After all, apart from the golf club, no other development had been permitted. To cut a long story short I started documenting what I saw. I discovered the truck belonged to a company run by Arthur Turner who, at the time, still owned the site. Before long a pattern appeared. The truck would enter the site every Tuesday and Thursday afternoon, stay for about an hour and then leave again. Eventually I plucked up the courage to sneak into the airfield one night. It was soon obvious that Mr Turner was using the site to dump hazardous waste, by the looks of it mainly old car batteries but also aluminium cans with screw tops. I opened one of these and found that they contained x-rays. There were also a number of yellow plastic bags with the words "DANGER, MEDICAL WASTE" written on them. I took photographs of everything and started compiling the dossier you have in front of you. I reported my findings to the environmental health department. A few weeks later I received a reply explaining that an officer had investigated the site but that no further action was going to be taken. I was disappointed but not surprised as Mr Turner was at that time the Council Leader. Soon after I was offered a job in Australia so I left the country for a number of years.

When, on my return, I heard about the New Town

development, I realised that my evidence could be important but decided to keep it quiet until the public consultation started, that way it would get maximum publicity.

At the same time I discovered lots of land being sold around the perimeter of the airbase. In itself not suspicious as the developer, Future Build, no doubt needed as much space as they could get. However, checking the land register, others had also been buying large parcels of land, years before the development started, only to sell to Future Build for a large profit at a later date. This sounded suspicious to me as very few people knew of the plans as far back as these acquisitions first started. Where did they get their information from? So far I have been unable to find out who is behind it all, other than that the transactions are completed using a firm of solicitors in Cambridge.

Steve put the letter down and, using his phone, took pictures of the evidence. He then placed the letter and photographs back in the box after which the bank manager and Alan put it back in its secure place.

'Thanks Alan,' said Steve while they were driving back along the A47. 'It will take some time to decipher it all but I'm pretty certain I now have a very good idea of who is behind Mr Evans' murder. I know, without you I wouldn't have all this information but I'd like to keep it confidential just for now if that's okay with you?'

Alan nodded.

'Don't worry,' he said, 'I already know too much for my liking. I'm the editor of a small local newspaper. I report on traffic accidents, council meetings, potholes and country fairs. Maybe when I was younger I might have dreamt of being a nationally known investigative journalist but those days are over. Nowadays I dream of retirement and joining the local opera society.'

'Fair enough,' said Steve, 'but I promise you, when all this is done and dusted, you'll be the first to be told.'

Chapter 23

Bob Bradley was in his office when his phone rang. It was Derk Pieters.

'What the fuck is going on?'

'We had to stop work again, they've found another body. But this one was murdered only recently.'

'What, the protester? I heard about it on the radio.'

'That's the one. Found in the same hole as the other guy. I don't know what to make of it all. I mean, these guys are a bit of a nuisance but why would anyone start murdering them?'

'I agree,' Pieters replied, 'I can't stand them but killing them doesn't do any of us any good. Tell me,' he said in a much less aggressive tone, 'what do you know about Arthur Turner?'

'A dinosaur from the past. Used to own the airfield site and probably really pissed off that we've more or less secured planning permission. He's been harassing one of the councillors I work with trying to stop the development. Why do you ask?'

'Nothing really, except that he came to see me wanting to employ the three guys working for my security company. And I've just heard that two of them have been arrested on suspicion of breaking and entering.'

Eva and PC Sheldon were making good time and found themselves in Peterborough just after two o'clock. They turned into the road where Mr and Mrs Trevelyan lived and stopped outside the house. An elderly gentleman was busy doing some weeding in the front garden.

'Mr Trevelyan?' Eva asked by way of a greeting.
'That's me, and you are?'
Eva showed her badge.
'I'd like a little chat.'
'Your colleague has already interviewed my wife. Why do you want to talk to us again?'
'I understand you had to leave before my colleague arrived. I just want to ask you about your memories.'
He got up.
'You're wasting your time but you'd better come in I suppose. Might as well get it over with. My wife is out I'm afraid.'
'That's okay, like I said, it's you we want to talk to.'
He led them around the side of the house to a smart patio.
'Do you mind sitting outside, it saves me having to change?'

It was a lovely day so they readily agreed.

'Thank you,' said Eva, 'I'm sorry to interrupt your gardening. What I would really like to know is what your feelings were around the time that the protests were taking place twenty-five years ago.'

'What do you mean *feelings*?'

'What did you think of it all?'

'Well, none of us wanted to have a nuclear waste dump on our doorstep so I agreed with opposing the planning application. But I was not happy with the actual protests. They called it nonviolent direct action but by doing that they were causing all of us a lot of problems.'

'What kind of problems?'

'Occasionally they would block the road which meant that the school bus couldn't pass. As a result many of the pupils would miss lessons. At other times the police would close the road if they were expecting problems.'

'And was that all?'

'No, it wasn't just that, it was also the way they looked and conducted themselves. Hygiene didn't seem high on their agenda, very few came from around here and I'm sure some of them stole potatoes and carrots from the farms. I was the headmaster of the local school and I thought they set a bad example for our children.'

'What made you change your mind? I mean you have now joined in the current protest against the New Town haven't you?'

'That's totally different. We are a group of responsible local people. Most of us are over fifty. We don't pull down fences or that sort of thing. Anyway, I don't have to justify myself to you.'

Eva could see that he was getting annoyed.

'Of course not, I'm just interested, that's all. Did you know any of the people who took part in the demonstrations at the time?'

'You mean personally?'

'Yes.'

'I wouldn't talk to them. Like I said, I didn't particularly like them. Also we were busy at the time. Our only daughter was getting married. A very good match too. Sadly it didn't last, as you well know.'

'Yet your daughter joined the protest did she not?'

'You're raking up some painful memories. What has my daughter's mistake to do with the fact that someone has been found murdered at the old airfield?'

'I'm not saying it has, but the more we know about that time the more likely we will find the murderer.'

'I tell you what I think. A couple of them will have got into an argument that got out of hand. No doubt the murderer soon left to go back to London or wherever he came from.'

'That's quite possible,' Eva agreed. 'Still, you haven't answered my question, did you know any of them personally? Did you talk to any of them?'

'Like I said, I avoided them.'

'Does the name Billy Gunn mean anything to you?'

'It does now,' was the answer. 'Anne told me he was the guy found dead at the airfield.'

'And you're sure you've never spoken to him? The discovery of the body has sparked a lot of gossip in the village. I know you live quite a long way away but have you heard anything that you think might be helpful to our enquiries?'

'I haven't spoken to anyone about this. It's none of my business. Really, I think you would have better things to do than bother a couple of old people. I'd like to get back to my gardening.'

'Of course, just one more question. Have you seen a picture of the victim?'

He nodded.

'Did you notice any similarities between the man in the picture and your grandson?'

Mr Trevelyan didn't speak but had turned bright red.

Please don't let him have a heart attack, Eva prayed, expecting him to explode in a rage of anger.

Instead Mr Trevelyan went very quiet before he eventually got up and spoke.

'Get out of my house. How dare you come here and spread filthy rumours about my daughter? Paul is Anne and Geoffrey's son and our grandson. Nothing more, nothing less. I will speak to your seniors. I can't for the life of me imagine why you think that Paul's parentage or otherwise has anything to do with a murder that happened twenty-five years ago.

Eva stood up to go.

'Neither can I,' she replied, 'at least not yet.'

By the time they arrived back at Downham Police Station Eva and PC Sheldon had had time to go over their talk with Mr Trevelyan.

'He was obviously lying when he said he hadn't talked about it with anyone,' says Eva, 'We already know from DI Woods that both parents had spoken to Anne and Geoffrey Henderson let slip that he and Mr Trevelyan had a phone conversation yesterday.'

PC Sheldon nodded.

'He was also lying when he said that he'd never been close to any of the protesters because his own daughter told Steve he had interrupted her and Billy.'

'How are you feeling?' Eva enquired. 'Have you got the energy for another visit? I'd like to hear what Anne has got to say for herself.'

'I'm in.'

'In that case I'll give her a ring.'

Alan Phelan was sitting in his office not sure what to do next. He wasn't lying when he told Steve he didn't really want to get involved but on reflection he realised he also had a duty to the readers of his paper to keep them up to date with developments. After all, murders were relatively rare in this area and to have two in exactly the same spot should make for a good story. And of course there was the effect it had on the progress of the New Town development. He picked up the phone and dialled Bob Bradley's number.

'Mr Bradley, Alan Phelan here from the Fenland Gazette. I'm interested to hear your reaction to the fact that two bodies have been found on the land you hope to develop.'

'I tell you what I think,' Bradley replied forcefully, 'I think the police and the authorities are taking the piss. They've shut us down for the second time. This is costing the company thousands of pounds in the short term and that's not even taking into account what it might mean to the whole development.'

'But surely, the police have no choice in the matter?'

'I think they do. They could have shut down just a small part and let us get on with our job.'

'How is the planning permission progressing?'

'That all seems fine, we just need to present a good case to the committee.'

'And you don't expect any problems?'

'Like what?' Bradley asked suspiciously, 'have you heard anything?'

Phelan took his time, not sure how much to say. He decided to take a risk.

'I have it on good authority that there might be an issue with contamination on the site.'

'What are you on about man, what sort of contamination?' Bradley demanded to know.

'Serious stuff. My source told me there was evidence of the airfield having been used as an illegal dumping site for dangerous waste materials. And then there's the rumour that some confidential information has been leaked allowing individuals to make large profits by buying up land cheaply only to sell it later once planning permission has been obtained.'

'Absolute codswallop. Whoever told you that is talking absolute rubbish and if you plan to print any of this crap I'll sue you and your useless rag for every penny you've got.'

With that he put the phone down.

Alan didn't know what to think. Did he reveal too much? Bradley sounded genuinely surprised. And how was he going to use all this information?

Bob Bradley did know what to do. The moment he had stopped talking to Alan Phelan he rang Anthony Fisher's mobile but it went straight to voicemail. So he rang the house instead. Saskia answered.

'Hi Bob,' she said, 'Anthony forgot to charge his phone. But he's downstairs, I'll give him a shout and he can pick up there.'

Bradley heard her calling out and a moment later Councillor Fisher answered the phone. Bradley got straight to the point and related his conversation with Alan Phelan. Fisher was quiet for a minute.

'Where did Phelan get all this from? Actually, never mind that. Is there any truth about the site being contaminated?'

'Of course not,' replied Bradley, 'I've never heard so much bollocks in my life. The whole place was thoroughly tested and examined twenty-five years ago and there was no sign of any contamination. Since then it has not been used. Our own inspection areas are also clean, you've seen the results.'

'But what about third parties buying up land?

Where does he get that from?'

'We better not discuss that over the phone,' Bradley suggested.

'I agree,' replied Fisher, 'but getting back to the contamination, surely, if we are certain the site is clean it doesn't matter whatever Alan Phelan prints.'

'Don't be so naive Fisher,' Bob Bradley growled. 'True or not true, it's the sort of thing that would get a lot of publicity and has the potential for the application to be postponed while further soil samples are taken. God, it might even mean the whole planning process has to start again and we simply don't have the money to wait much longer. As for the other thing, ask Saskia if she's free to meet us for lunch tomorrow. We need a plan of action.'

Just after Anthony Fisher put the phone down he heard his wife coming down the stairs.

'Hi love,' he greeted her, 'Bob Bradley wondered if you were free to meet us tomorrow for lunch? Apparently, Alan Phelan from the local paper is taking an interest in some land deals in the area. Bob thinks, and I agree, that we had better prepare ourselves for questions being asked.'

'Of course,' Saskia replied. 'I listened in to the conversation. Why don't you ring Bob back and say we can meet at my office in Cambridge.'

The two employees from *POSH Security* were driven to Downham Market in two different squad cars. This gave DI Woods and DS Newman a chance to discuss what they had learnt. Before long Simon decided to ring the station and bring DCS Sutton and Steve up to date. So by the time they arrived at the police station it didn't take long before they were ready to formally interview the two men.

Steve and Sergeant Newman sat in front of the younger of the two. After informing him of his rights Steve nodded to his colleague to start the tape. The man confirmed his name and stated that he didn't need a solicitor.

'I know I'm in trouble,' he told the detectives, 'but I've had enough. I took the job because it was good money and I was led to believe all we would do was surveillance and gathering evidence. No one said anything about breaking into houses or kidnapping people.'

'Ah yes, tell us about the kidnap,' Steve said, hoping his voice didn't betray that he had no idea what the other man was talking about.

'We were told to collect the younger Mr Evans and deliver him to Peterborough. We were supposed to meet him outside Greggs in Downham Market but when he saw us it looked as if he was going to run away so I forced him into the car. We were told to take him to a flat in Peterborough and keep him there until he had told us everything he knew. But after a few hours the boss rang and said he wasn't happy and that we were to wait. Then Charlie turned up and he took over.'

'Who is Charlie?'

'Our manager.'

'And what happened then?'

'We were told to go to Mr Evans' house and try to find a key to a safety deposit box.'

'And what happened when you got there?'

'Well, we started looking around and old Mr Evans must have woken up and he came downstairs. He started shouting. I told him to shut up but he wouldn't. He ran back up the stairs but fell and rolled down a few steps, that's how he hurt himself.'

'What happened to young Mr Evans?'

'I have no idea, we left him with Charlie.'

They took a break and were sitting in DCS Sutton's office comparing notes. Both men had told more or less the same story.

'Strange,' remarked Sarah, 'you'd think they would put up more resistance. The guy we interviewed seemed convinced that we had plenty of evidence against him.'

'Same with our guy,' Steve concurred, 'I wonder why that is?'

'I think that might be my doing.' DI Woods admitted. 'I made them believe that Mr Evans senior was well enough to identify them.'

'In that case I truly hope Mr Evans pulls through,' replied DCS Sutton and, looking directly at Simon she added, 'especially for your sake. There are a lot of loose ends to tie up and I suggest we need to interview them in depth again tomorrow. For now though can I take it we believe them when they say they don't know what happened to Mr Evans after this mysterious Charlie took over?'

They all agreed.

'In that case finding Charlie must be our main priority. And his boss.'

'I think that is most likely our old friend Derk Pieters,' DI Woods said.

'Derk Pieters indeed,' Steve replied, 'now why doesn't that surprise me.' He thought back to a previous case where Mr Pieters had been implemented in pulling the strings behind a number of incidents. Nothing could be proved however and he'd walked away scot free.'

'You know,' he said, looking at the clock. 'If we leave now we could be in Peterborough by five o'clock. Get your coat Simon, we're going to visit a brothel.'

They got to the address in Peterborough at the same time that Derk Pieters was just about to enter the building.

'Detective Chief Inspector, what a pleasure to see you again,' Pieters greeted Steve. 'And you of course too,' he gestured at DI Woods.

'What can I do for you, don't tell me it's a coincidence. Come inside, I'll get us some coffee.'

They followed Pieters up the stairs to the area he called his Club but which all three men knew was better described as a brothel. It being early there didn't seem to be anyone else in the building. Pieters seemed to read their thoughts.

'My secretary is downstairs. Sadly my trusted lieutenant is spending some time on holiday in Norwich prison, thanks to you.'

'How is Teddy?' Steve enquired, remembering how the man with the inappropriate nickname had been found guilty of manslaughter a year before.

'You know what,' Pieters laughed, 'I really must go and visit him one of these days. But you know what it's like …'

'I don't,' said Steve, 'but never mind, I understand you own the security agency next door.'

'I do,' Pieters agrees, 'on paper anyway. I leave the day to day running up to the manager, Charlie Engledow. But my secretary does the books for

POSH Security. What is all this about if I may ask?'

'We have reason to believe that some of your employees have been involved in criminal activity and we need to speak to Mr Engledow as a matter of urgency. You don't know where I can find him do you?'

'I do as a matter of fact. He should be here any minute. He's asked to see me because two of his staff have been arrested. But then you knew that of course,' he challenged the detectives.

Steve ignored the remark.

'And what do you know about the case they are, or rather were, working on?'

'Absolutely nothing,' replied Pieters, 'in fact I'm keen to find out myself. You see,' he says, 'a week ago I was made a generous offer from an anonymous person who needed the exclusive use of three men to carry out delicate undercover surveillance on his bchalf. As there are only three employees and we didn't have much else on, I offered him the whole lot, office included.'

'And you don't know who this person is?'

'No, he was adamant he wanted to stay anonymous. I respect that.'

'How would you be paid?'

'In cash, in fact he paid £5,000 up front with the same sum due tomorrow.'

At that moment the bell rang. Pieters got up.

'Stay where you are,' Steve told him. 'DI Woods and I will meet him downstairs. Thanks for your time, no doubt we'll speak again soon. In fact, I'd like you to attend a voluntary interview tomorrow morning at ten o'clock.'

Pieters looked perplexed at this sudden change in attitude from the detectives.

'Will I need my solicitor?' he asked.

'That,' DCI Culverhouse replied, 'is up to you.' With that they made their way downstairs where they confronted Mr Engledow who was too surprised to put up any resistance when he was told he was being arrested on suspicion of kidnap and murder. They summoned the squad car which had been waiting discreetly round the corner and before long they were on their way to Downham Market Police Station.

Chapter 23

Eva and PC Sheldon were a little early. Anne Trevelyan told them she would be available from eight o'clock onwards. This gave the two police officers an hour to get something to eat and to discuss strategy. They decided to go to one of the fast food restaurants recently opened on the Ely bypass.

'What do you know about her?' Ben Sheldon asked.

'You already know the family relations. What Anne has told Steve is that she had an affair with one of the protesters even though she was about to get married. After the marriage she was going to move to Oundle. One day she decided to say goodbye to her lover at the camp but he was no longer there. I don't think she had made a connection between his disappearance and the news that a body had been found until she heard the murdered person was called Billy Gunn. Apparently she broke down.
Sarah also believes that she immediately understood the implication of this discovery because the

murdered man may well have been her son Paul's father. We are waiting for a DNA test to confirm this.'

'So why are we seeing her tonight?' PC Sheldon asked.

'As far as I see it, if the fact that Anne was pregnant with Billy's baby was known to her father, her ex-husband and herself, all three would have had a motive to keep this quiet.'

'But surely, murder is a bit extreme isn't it?'

'Absolutely, but it might not have been planned. Maybe one, or even two of them, approached Billy and things got out of hand.'

'I think you might be right, but how are we going to prove any of this?'

'I'm not sure,' Eva admitted. 'Let's just hope that our interview with Anne throws some unexpected light on the case. '

With that they left the restaurant and made their way to the village of Black Fen Drove.

Steve and DI Woods had stopped for some fish and chips in Outwell so by the time they arrived back in Downham, Charlie Engledow was already sitting in the interview room looking nervous. He was flanked by the same solicitor Steve remembered from his previous dealings with Mr Pieters.

DCS Sutton was waiting for them.

'I'd like to join you,' she said.

After the formalities had been completed the solicitor spoke first,

'Before we start please tell me on what grounds you have arrested my client?'

'Mr Engledow is, as far as we know, the last person who saw Mr Evans alive.'

'Being the last person to see someone alive is not a crime.'

'No,' agreed Steve, 'but kidnapping and false imprisonment is. And we have witnesses to testify that your client accepted responsibility for Mr Evans in exactly that scenario.'

The solicitor looked at Charlie Engledow.

'Can we have a few minutes?' she asked.

'Of course.'

DI Woods stopped the recording and the detectives left the room.

'She's obviously not properly briefed,' said DCS Sutton, 'Hopefully that will be to our advantage.'

When they returned they were greeted by a question.

'What evidence do you have that my client was part of any such kidnapping plot.'

'Like I said, we have two witnesses. In addition the room where Mr Evans was held is being checked for fingerprints and all CCTV footage from in and outside the building is being examined.'

Mr Engledow looked up.

'You're right,' he said, 'I was there. But I only spent a few hours with him and that was that.'

'What do you mean, that was that?'

'I was told to get Mr Evans down to the old airfield.'

'Told by whom?'

'The guy I work for.'

'Mr Pieters?'

'No, Mr Pieters is my real boss but I was working for this other guy. But I never met him. He gave his instructions by phone. While we were in the room this guy spoke to Mr Evans on the speaker phone. He asked him where the key to a safety deposit box was. Mr Evans told him he didn't have it on him but that he could get it before the bank opened the following day. I was told to check his pockets but he told the truth, he didn't have it.'

Steve produced a phone they confiscated when they arrested Mr Engledow.

'Is this the phone you used?'

'Yes.'

The detective was pleased to see that it was his personal phone, rather than a one off, non-traceable pay as you go. Hopefully the caller also used his own.

'Thank you, we will get it back to you when we've finished with it. Tell me what happened at the airfield?'

'I received a message telling me to drop him at the far gate near the old control tower.'

That's where the body was found Steve realised.

'And then?'

'I had to get out of the car and both Mr Evans and I were to face the road. I heard someone behind us and then this guy told Mr Evans that he had a gun and to turn around and face him. He told me to stay where I was. I recognised the voice. It was the same as the one who rang me, the one who told me what to do on the phone. I heard nothing more so after a few minutes I turned around but they'd disappeared. I ran back to the car and got out of there as quickly as I could.'

'Why didn't you ring the police?'

'Like I said, he had a gun. I don't know who *he* is but he definitely knows who *I* am and most likely knows where I live too!'

Sarah and Steve were having a coffee in her office. It was getting late, nearly nine o'clock. They'd decided to call it a day and to resume the interviews with the three men in the morning when they might have some news from the phone records.

'What do you think?' Sarah asked Steve.

'We're very close,' he said. 'Presuming that the three men downstairs are telling the truth we are literally only one step away from arresting the murderer. Let's hope the phone records will give us some solid evidence.'

'Any ideas?' Sarah asked.

'I have,' said Steve, 'but it's unlikely the guy I've got in mind would get his own hands dirty. But we'll see. Sarah didn't push it further. '

'I wonder how Eva is getting on.'

'I haven't heard from her all day,' replied Steve.

'I briefly saw her at the station earlier on. She told me she and PC Sheldon had an appointment to see Anne Trevelyan tonight,' Sarah said, before adding,

'we better get some rest. I think tomorrow might be a busy day'.

Steve was looking forward to a shower, a whiskey and bed but before he arrived home his phone rang. It was Alan Phelan.

'I'm really sorry detective but I've just had a text telling me to meet someone at the airfield near the old control tower at eleven-thirty tonight.'

Steve looked at his watch.

'That's in two hours' time. Who was the text from and what do they want?'

'I asked that question. Apparently, whoever it is, has some explosive revelations about what's been happening with the planning application. But rather than talking on the phone or by email this person reckoned it was something they needed to show me in person.'

'Any idea what they are talking about?'

'No, not really, but I wouldn't be surprised if it has something to do with the dangerous waste buried there.'

'Are you going?'

'I am, I just wanted you to know.'

'Thanks,' Steve said, 'take care.'

He paused, 'actually, on second thoughts I'll follow you. Just to make sure it's not some kind of trap.'

Alan let out an audible sigh of relief.

'I was hoping you'd say that,' he replied.

When Eva and Ben arrived at Anne Trevelyan's house they noticed another car in the drive. Anne opened the door and asked them to follow her to the living room where they were surprised to be greeted by Anne's parents.

'Hello again,' said Mr Trevelyan. 'Anne rang us and told us you were coming so we are here to offer our daughter moral support.'

Eva was struck by how tall both parents appeared next to their daughter.

'There was no need father,' Anne said, obviously slightly embarrassed by her parents' presence. 'I am a grown woman and can look after myself.'

'I don't want to hear of it Anne,' he dismissed her comment. 'We're just here to make sure they don't put words into your mouth. After all, these two officers are obviously fairly inexperienced.' And, looking at Eva he added, 'no offence.'

Eva felt herself getting angry. First the ex-husband, now the parents. What was it with this family?

'It's understandable that you are concerned about your daughter but we have come to speak to Anne alone.'

Looking at Anne she asked 'Is there somewhere your parents can go?'

'The kitchen I suppose.'

In spite of Mr Trevelyan's protestations the two elderly people soon left the room.

'I'm sorry about that,' Anne said. 'I told them not to come but you know what parents are like.'

'Don't worry,' replied Eva, 'my dad would probably have been exactly the same.'

'Ms Trevelyan…'

'Please, call me Anne.'

'Okay Anne, we know you've already told DCI Culverhouse and DCS Sutton most of what you know but I have a few further questions. Some are rather personal. Is that okay?'

Anne nodded.

'We are trying to establish a motive for the murder of William Gunn also known as Billy. I understand you had an intimate relationship with him. Is that correct?'

'It is,' Anne answered, 'but I knew it wouldn't lead to anything. I was already engaged to be married.'

'Did anyone else know about your relationship with Mr Gunn?'

'I don't think so, I mean, I'm sure some of the other people at the camp might have done but as far as I am concerned we were being very discreet.'

'Why did you feel the need to be discreet?'

'Think about it, like I said, I was already engaged to someone else. You've met my father, how do you think he would have reacted if he'd found out? Let alone my future husband. Don't forget my parents thought my marriage to Geoffrey was a gift from heaven.'

'Why was that?'

'In spite of my father's education and position he always suffered from the fact that his parents had been dirt poor farm workers. Geoffrey represented everything he wanted for his daughter. A public school educated son from a prominent old and rich established farming family. I could not let him down.'

'But your father did find out didn't he?'

'Yes he did. One day he drove past and saw us. He was very angry.'

'Did your fiancé ever find out?'

'I don't think so. If he did he never mentioned it although ….'

She paused.

'Geoffrey was very possessive. At the time I saw that as a sign of his commitment to me but once we were married it started to irritate. It was one of the reasons I left him. He kept saying, "How do I know I can trust you?" I didn't know what he meant at the time but now I wonder if he had heard something.'

'Was he ever violent towards you?'

'Oh no, he would raise his voice every now and then and when I told him I was leaving him he got very angry and upset but he never physically threatened me.'

'DCS Sutton who interviewed you suggested that you now realise Mr Gunn, Billy, could be your son's father.'

Anne nodded.

'Is this the first time you have thought this?'

Anne didn't answer.

'Sorry,' Eva said. 'I realise this must be painful for you. We'll soon leave you alone, just one more question.'

'How would you describe your relationship with Mr Gunn?'

'What do you mean exactly?'

'Was it a fling? Was it an affair? Was it passionate?'

Anne started crying.

'It wasn't any of those things or maybe it was all of them.' She paused and then whispered, 'I loved him.'

'And, had you known that he was Paul's father, would you still have married Geoffrey?'

'To be honest, I've always known deep inside that Billy was Paul's father. I just didn't want to admit it to myself. Please don't repeat this but when I told your colleagues that I went to say goodbye to Billy that wasn't the whole truth. I had packed my bag and was willing to follow him to wherever. But as you know, he had already left.'

She was quiet for a moment. 'And now we know why.' By now the tears were streaming down her face.

'Thank you very much,' Eva said, putting her hand on Anne's arm. In doing so she touched the charm bracelet Anne was wearing.

'Oh that's lovely,' she said, admiring the different patterned charms.

'My mum made it for me,' Anne said through her

tears. 'She gave it to me for my eighteenth birthday. It symbolises our eternal love. She made it herself on a jewellery course.'

'That's so sweet,' replied Eva, relieved that Anne had calmed down a bit. 'I'm really sorry we've had to put you through all this.' They got up. 'Don't worry, we'll see ourselves out.'

They quietly closed the front door and walked to their car but just when they were about to get in two cars drove past on the narrow road. She recognised the second one as Steve's. What was he doing here? She decided to text him.

Hey, you nearly ran me over just now, what are you doing such a long way from home at this time of the night?

Immediately her phone rang.

'Eva, are you on your own?'

'No, I've got PC Sheldon with me.'

'So much the better. I can't explain just now but do me a favour. Can you park, out of the way, somewhere near the old control tower entrance to the airfield? Turn your lights off. I'll call you there.'

The line went dead.

'What was that all about?' asked Sheldon.

'God knows.'

Chapter 24

As soon as Alan Phelan arrived at the airfield his phone pinged. It was a text message telling him to park his car near the gate and walk towards the old control tower. He rang Steve and told him about the text.

'You go,' Steve suggested, 'don't worry, I won't be far behind.'

Alan was nervous but did what he was told. When he arrived he found the gate open. He got out of his car and, illuminated by the moonlight, saw a figure dressed in black and wearing a balaclava waiting for him at the base of the tower. Holding a mobile the person gestured for Alan to get his phone out as well. Immediately he received a text.

I have with me a bag containing twenty thousand pounds. It is all yours if you stop your investigation and don't publicise anything you think you might know.

Alan was shocked and perplexed. He felt he was in a film. This sort of thing didn't happen to people like him. He was definitely tempted. He was still a few years off retirement. This would help. He replied, *I need to think about it.*

An immediate response,

You've got five minutes.

After a little while the person walked towards him with the bag.

'And?'

Alan was surprised. He recognised the voice but couldn't place it. 'I'm sorry,' he said, 'I can't do it.'

'You fool,' came the reply and before he knew what was happening he was pushed into the same hole where William Gunn's and Richard Evans' bodies were found.

He got up, realised he was not injured, and tried to climb out of the hole. Suddenly he heard an engine and the sound of a tractor or something similar approaching. The first bucket of soil took him by surprise. He realised what was happening and panicked. He was being buried alive.

Next thing he knew he was screaming for help but there was no one to hear him. The second bucket came raining down on him. He tried to scramble out but one of his feet was stuck in the soil. It was only a matter of time before his whole body would be covered.

'Please stop,' he pleaded.

But the digger kept coming.

While Steve was waiting for Alan to return he started to feel increasingly uneasy. But even so he held back for a while. But then curiosity got the better of him and he made his way quietly in the direction of the old control tower. When he arrived it took him a few seconds to realise what was happening. Using his radio he quickly called for immediate back up and ran over to the digger.

The driver noticed him and tried to turn the machine around to block his path. But Steve had already jumped onto the step used to get up to the cab. The driver started moving the digger forward and backward making sudden stops and unexpected jerks in an attempt to throw the detective off. Suddenly Steve was aware of someone else jumping onto the digger on the other side of the cab. It was PC Sheldon. The driver was now panicking and turned to look around. Steve seized the moment to open the door and with a mighty leap threw himself inside, knocking the driver sideways. He had just about enough time to turn the engine off before he received an almighty punch. For a moment he felt as if he was going to lose his balance but PC Sheldon had opened the other door and had managed to put a handcuff on the driver's wrist, securing the other one to the steering wheel. By now the whole area was lit up by the light of at least four police cars who had

all answered the call for urgent assistance.
Steve shouted down to Eva.

'We're alright, help him,' and pointed at the hole where a petrified Alan Phelan was standing, half buried in the soil.

'Whoever you are,' Steve told the driver, 'your game is over. Consider yourself under arrest.'

To his surprise a female voice growled at him:

'Fuck off.'

She removed the balaclava and Steve found himself face to face with a very angry Saskia Fisher.

Even though it was well after midnight, all the lights at the police station were on when Steve and the other officers arrived back. After Saskia was put in the back of one of the squad cars, Steve had rung DCS Sutton who had already gone to bed. She immediately got dressed and met them in the car park.

'Well,' said Steve, 'that was a bit of a surprise.'

'Come inside,' replied Sarah Sutton. 'It looks like you can all do with a strong coffee.'

Once seated Steve started telling what had happened. He finished by singling out Ben Sheldon.

'If this guy hadn't been there, the outcome could have been quite different.'

'Well done,' agreed Sarah.

PC Sheldon looked embarrassed but it was obvious that he was chuffed to be praised like that by the two senior officers.

'Thank you,' he said, 'I'm sure you would have managed on your own.'

'What about Mr Phelan?'

'He's in Addenbrooks hospital,' replied Eva. 'To be quite honest, once we got him out of the hole, he didn't look too bad but I'm sure it will take a bit of time before he forgets the ordeal he went through.'

'And what about Mrs Fisher?'

'The ambulance crew checked her over. She's fine. We've charged her with attempted murder and resisting a police officer. She's been offered a solicitor but she told us she'll think about it. I am waiting for her husband to arrive any minute. We've sent two officers round to their house. I've told them that if he doesn't come willingly they are to arrest him.'

Just then Eva's phone rang.

'It's one of the officers,' she said. 'Apparently Anthony Fisher is not at home, or at least he isn't answering the door.' She handed her phone to Steve.

'When did you start your shift?' he asked the officer.

'Ten o'clock, we're on nights.'

'In that case I'd like you to stay where you are just

in case he's hiding or arriving home late.'

DCS Sutton got up.

'Can I suggest we quickly have a preliminary interview with Mrs Fisher and then try and get a couple of hours' sleep?'

'Good idea,' said Steve, 'I've had it for today. Well done everyone. See you all bright and early.'

While Steve and DCS Sutton made their way to the cells, Eva and PC Sheldon were walking to the car park.

'Enough excitement for you?' Eva laughed.

'You know what, I know it probably sounds odd, but I've really enjoyed myself these last few days.'

'I know exactly what you mean,' replied Eva.

'Goodnight.'

Steve felt he was in luck. Saskia Fisher had told them that they were wasting their time. She was not going to talk to them until she had spoken to her husband. Steve handed her his phone.

'Feel free to ring him and if he answers ask him where he is?'

She keyed in the number.

No reply.

She left a message telling her husband to get to the police station as soon as possible.

'We'll continue our conversation tomorrow,' Steve promised.

'Whatever.'

He arrived home half an hour later and looked at his watch; three o'clock.

He poured himself a whiskey thinking he needed to wind down. But before he knew it, he fell into a deep, deep sleep.

By eight o'clock the next morning the whole team had gathered in the incident room. DCS Sutton started by recounting the events from the night before for the benefit of Sergeant Newman and DI Woods.

'So we missed all the fun,' remarked Simon Woods, sounding disappointed.

'At least you got some sleep,' whispered Eva.

'Okay,' Sarah continued. 'This case is getting more complicated by the minute. We now have four suspects in the cells, all charged with either murder or other violent offences. We know that the common factor is something to do with the airfield. DC Lappinska, I want you and PC Sheldon to put the Billy Gunn case to one side for the time being and concentrate on recent developments. Ben,' she addressed PC Sheldon, 'I seem to remember you are a bit of a whizz-kid when it comes to computers. Can you see if you can detect any patterns or similarities that could be useful to us please?'

'I'd be happy to.'

She nodded to Steve.

'Thank you,' he said. 'One of the things that interests me is that we have four suspects and two major crimes. I am curious to know if this is the end of it or if there are others involved. One person I'm particularly interested in talking to is Arthur Turner. He was mentioned by Richard Evans as someone who had a vested interest for the New Town development to be stopped because he had used the site in the past for dumping hazardous waste. DI Woods and Sergeant Newman, I'd like you to surprise him at home. Take some uniformed officers with you. Ask him to come to the station on a voluntary basis. If he refuses, arrest him on suspicion of illegal waste dumping and involvement in murder. And make sure you immediately confiscate his phone. We will try to get a search warrant ASAP and email it to you.'

'What are we looking for?' asked DI Woods.

'His phone and any shoes or boots you can find.'

Soon everybody was on their way. Just then Maddie rang and told Steve there was a visitor to see him.

'I'm expecting Derk Pieters any moment,' he said to DCS Sutton by way of explanation. 'If we're not careful we're going to be short of cell space before long.'

He made his way downstairs. But it wasn't Derk Pieters waiting for him in the foyer, it was a very nervous Mr Fisher.

'What is all this about?' He addressed Steve. 'I had a message from my wife to come here but I didn't read it until this morning. What am I doing here and where's my wife? Is she alright?'

'Let's sit down,' Steve suggested, 'and I will explain everything to you.' They made their way to one of the interview rooms.

'Take a seat Mr Fisher. Before we start, can I ask you where you were last night?'

'I was in Peterborough for a meeting. I had a few drinks so I decided to stay at a colleague's house. I tried to ring Saskia but she didn't answer her phone. Then I saw her message this morning. Tell me what's happened? Has she been in an accident?'

Steve noticed there was real panic in his voice. If he was aware of his wife's antics last night he was hiding it very well.

'Your wife has not had an accident, however, before we go any further, what time did you leave home yesterday?'

Fisher looked slightly more relaxed.

'Between four and five in the afternoon sometime. We had a cup of tea and a chat and then I left.

'So your wife was still at home by five o'clock?' Steve suggested.

'As far as I know, yes, I don't think she had any plans to go out. Can you now please tell me what's happening?'

'Thanks,' said Steve. 'Okay Mr Fisher, your wife has been arrested for attempted murder and obstructing a police officer. She is currently being held here at the station.'

Anthony Fisher looked dumb struck.

'No,' he said, 'that can't be right. Saskia? Attempted murder? You must have arrested the wrong person.'

'I'm afraid we haven't, 'answered Steve. 'Under the circumstances I have to ask you to remain here for the next few hours as my colleagues and I will have further questions for you.'

Fisher was now clearly getting angry.

'You can't do this to me or my wife,' he said. 'Do you know who I am? I demand to speak to your boss.'

'That can be arranged,' answered Steve. 'She is looking forward to meeting you too.'

He had just finished telling Sarah about his meeting with the councillor when Derk Pieters arrived, together with his solicitor.

'Thanks for coming,' Steve greeted him.

'Didn't seem like I had much choice.'

'What are the charges?' the solicitor wanted to know.

'No charges yet,' Steve replied, 'just questions. For a start I would like to know where you were last night?'

'I was at a presentation with a number of councillors in Peterborough,' he answered.

'Was one of them Anthony Fisher?'

'Yes he was there, I didn't speak to him though.'

'What was the meeting about?'

'Changes to the structure of planning regulations in the light of new Government proposals.'

'Sounds interesting.'

'You must be joking. It was boring as hell. I only went because some of it might just be relevant to a housing development I'm involved in.'

'I see,' Steve replied. 'I didn't know you were involved in that line of work?'

'I am a major shareholder in Future Build,' Pieters replied proudly.

'You mean the company behind the proposed New Town?'

'The very same.'

'And how is that going?'

'It was going great until your lot kept finding bodies which meant the work had to stop again!'

'Did you know the victim, Mr Evans?'

'No I did not, although I've obviously read about him since. I feel sorry for the guy. I mean I have no

time for his politics but....'
He paused,

'Wait a minute, you don't think I've got anything to do with his murder do you?'

'We have three of your employees in custody who have admitted being involved in the kidnapping of Mr Evans. One of them has even confessed that his boss told him to drive the poor guy to the airfield where he was murdered. And as you are his boss...'

'I would like a few minutes with my client,' the solicitor told Steve.'

'Of course,'

'No need,' said Pieters. 'You're right, I am their boss but as I already told you, all three were working for someone else.'

'Oh yes, the mysterious man who pays cash. You haven't remembered his name by any chance have you? It would make me much more inclined to believe you.'

'Okay,' Pieters said, 'it's Turner, Arthur Turner.'

At the same time that Steve was talking to Derk Pieters, Sergeant Newman and DI Woods were remonstrating with Arthur Turner outside his front door.

'Get off my land,' the older man shouted. 'You have no right to be here.'

'We are police officers and have the right to demand you come with us to the station.'

'I'm calling my solicitor,' Turner shouted and turned around to go back into the house.

'You do that,' Simon suggested, 'and you can tell him that you are being arrested on suspicion of murder.'

Turner turned around again.

'Have you gone absolutely mad?'

He got out his mobile and dialled a number. DI Woods decided to let him make the call.

'Yes,' they heard Turner explain, 'they think I've murdered someone. When can you be here? That's great.'

He turned around to face the detectives.

'My solicitor will be here in ten minutes. He's told me not to talk to you.' DI Woods' phone pinged.

It was an email from DCS Sutton with the search warrant attached. He showed it to Sergeant Newman. This was going to be fun. He beckoned over some of the uniformed officers who so far had kept their distance.

'Get ready for an initial search of the house,' he said. 'Concentrate on finding his boots and shoes and any other mobile phones he may have. Don't forget to check inside his car.'

The solicitor arrived. DI Woods walked towards him

and showed him the warrant.

'You will have plenty of time to speak to your client once we are at the station but I must ask you to let us do our job first and that is to search the premises and transport Mr Turner to Downham Market.'

The solicitor read the warrant and walked over to Arthur Turner.

'Don't worry,' he said, 'we'll sort this but for now you have no choice but to accompany the officers to the police station. I will meet you there.'

Turner suddenly looked like a man who had lost all fight in him.

'Okay,' he said when DI Woods asked him to hand over his mobile and before long they made their way back to Downham Market.

By two o'clock in the afternoon the whole team was assembled in the incident room. Sarah thanked everybody and explained to the others that they had interviewed the employees from *POSH Security* again but that they had stuck to the same story. In other words they admitted their part in breaking in to Mr Evans' house and kidnapping his son but denied any knowledge or involvement in the murder. The same went for Charlie Engledow. He admitted handing over Mr Evans to an anonymous third party but denied knowing anything about what happened after that.

'I actually think I believe them,' she concluded. 'But we'll see.'

Steve explained about his interview with Derk Pieters.

'However much I dislike the man,' he said, 'I think that on this occasion he is speaking the truth. But I'm keeping an open mind.'

They turned to the subject of Anthony Fisher and his wife.

We've checked his story out and it is true that he was nowhere near the airfield when his wife attacked poor Mr Phelan.'

'How is he?' someone asked.

'I spoke to him this morning,' Eva said. 'He's a lot better and thanks everybody for rescuing him.'

'That's good to hear,' replied Steve. 'How did you and PC Sheldon get on?'

Eva nodded to her colleague.

'It's complicated,' said Ben. 'From what I can see there are two distinct patterns. First there are those who want the New Town to go ahead at all costs. They include Mr and Mrs Fisher.'

'But why try to kill Mr Phelan?' DCS Sutton asked.

'I think I know,' Steve said. 'Mrs Fisher somehow

got wind of the fact that Alan Phelan was doing an investigation into the whole thing. She needed to silence him or she would lose a lot of money.'

'In what way?' DI Woods asked.

Steve nodded to Ben Sheldon.

'I found out that the company in Cambridge that has been the front for buying up land around the airfield, belongs to Mrs Fisher. It is registered in her maiden name but it's definitely her. So I put two and two together and presume she got the confidential information about the plans from her husband who is a prominent councillor. But so far I have no clear proof.'

'Brilliant work,' DCS Sutton said. 'It means that even if we can't prove the councillor was involved with the attack on Mr Phelan, we can most likely do him for fraud. Thanks Ben, well done.'

PC Sheldon beamed. That was twice in two days he'd received praise from the top boss.

'And the second strand?' she continued.

'Those who want to stop the development at all costs.'

'You mean the environmental campaigners?'

'Yes but not just them. In terms of the murder of Mr Evans it is more likely that they were concerned he would reveal the dumping of illegal waste. Even though that in itself would be enough to halt the plans which they would like, it would also mean that the person responsible for the waste would be exposed as a major polluter. That person's reputation would take a severe knock.'

More praise, this time from Steve,

'Thanks Ben, excellent work.'

'You think this person is Mr Turner? Sarah asked Steve.

'I do,' he said, 'and with more evidence coming in by the minute I think it's time to have a chat with him. See you all back here at five o'clock. Good work everyone, start writing up those reports.'

In the end the interview with Mr Turner didn't take that long. His footprints were literally all over the murder. The phone calls to the *POSH Security* employees were made from his mobile. The imprint of the sole at the crime scene matched his expensive Kestrel Country Boots. Derk Pieters identified him as his mystery client and the evidence put together by Richard Evans was more than enough to trigger off a full scale investigation into what kind of waste had been dumped at the site over the years.

He was adamant however that he had no choice.

'I offered Evans a way out but he refused to accept it. I said I would double the money I had already given him if he let the matter go. He insulted me, called me a capitalist pig and all sorts. At one point I thought he was coming for me. He didn't know, but my gun had no bullets in it. But when he got close I hit him over the head. He fell over so I dragged him to the hole and dropped him in it. To be quite honest, he got what he deserved. These so-called greens and lefties, all they do is stop ordinary businessmen like me from making an honest living.'

The mood at the five o'clock meeting was remarkably upbeat except for the fact that they had just been informed that Mr Evans senior had died from his injuries. Probably for the best Steve thought. DCS Sutton read out the main points from a press statement she would release the next day.

Arthur Turner has been charged with the murder of Richard Evans. His company has been referred to Environmental Health who have promised to carry out a thorough investigation. They have already taken the first step in closing the airfield site until further notice.

The two POSH Security employees have been charged with breaking and entering, kidnap and false imprisonment. A further charge of manslaughter might be added.

Charlie Engledow is charged with false imprisonment and withholding evidence of a crime from the police.

Saskia Fisher has been charged with attempted murder and resisting arrest.

She explained to the others that the evidence against Anthony Fisher and his wife relating to the land deals had been handed to the Serious Fraud Office. Both were likely to face further charges but this had not been included in the press release.

After everyone had left, Sarah and Steve were having a final debrief in her office.
'That was a job well done,' said Steve.
'I agree, however, I have one more bit of bad news I didn't want to make public just yet.'
Steve looked concerned.
'I've received a letter from DI Starling. She has asked for indefinite leave to look after her mother. I've contacted Human Resources and told them we have no objections.'
'That's a bit of a blow,' said Steve, 'it will leave us seriously short but …'
'Are you thinking what I'm thinking,' asked DCS Sutton.

'I think so,' answered Steve. 'Young Ben Sheldon has done remarkably well. I think we should snap him up before anyone else does.'

'My thoughts exactly,' replied Sarah.

Chapter 25

Steve and Eva had agreed to meet at the small Indian restaurant in town for a celebratory meal. When he arrived she was already waiting on the bench near the town clock. Steve noticed that she was looking a little glum. Probably tired he thought, he definitely was. Before long they were seated and enjoying a glass of wine. They recalled the events of the last few weeks and agreed that it had been quite a case. Steve raised his glass.

'On a successful outcome,' he said.
Eva did the same but Steve couldn't help noticing that her heart obviously wasn't in it.

'What is it?' he wanted to know. 'I can tell something is wrong.'

'I don't know,' Eva replied. 'It probably sounds stupid but everyone has done such a good job in catching these criminals, I sort of feel I've rather let the side down.'

'Whatever do you mean?'

'We still haven't found out who murdered Mr Gunn' she replied.

'We probably never will. But if it helps, I'm aware that we haven't had a proper debrief. Why don't we eat first and then you can talk me through the case so far.'

'I'd like that,' she replied.

The food arrived and both were quiet while enjoying the delicious taste of two perfectly cooked Paneer Saag curries.

'Start at the beginning,' Steve suggested when the waiter had cleared the table.'

'Well you know most of it really,' said Eva. 'I'm sure you must have concluded that the main suspects were either Anne herself, her ex-husband or her father.

Steve nodded.

'The problem is that murder seems a very extreme way to deal with the situation, even though I can understand why they might have wanted Billy Gunn out of their lives.'

She continued.

'After interviewing Anne I have discounted her as a suspect. I actually believe that given the chance she would have chosen Mr Gunn over her husband.'

'That leaves Mr Trevelyan and her ex-husband,' said Steve.

'I know,' said Eva. 'It could be either of them or it could be both. But I have nothing to link them to the murder scene. I've re-read the pathologists report twice but I can't seem to find any clues.'

'Maybe we'll have to accept that we'll never find out,' said Steve. 'But don't beat yourself up over it. It wasn't for want of effort on your part.'

'You're right,' Eva said, 'I'm sorry, I'm just super sensitive. Coffee?'

They agreed and before long a waitress arrived and put a tray in front of Eva who noticed the bracelet she was wearing.

'That's lovely, where did you get it?'

'In Peterborough,' she answered and mentioned the name of the shop.

'They make all their own jewellery on the premises,' she added.

'Thank you.'

Eva turned to Steve.

'Will you excuse me for a minute?' said Eva and stepped outside. Steve could see her checking her phone through the window. Five minutes later she was back.

'I know who murdered Billy Gunn,' she said.

When Eva and Steve arrived in Peterborough the next morning it was clear that the Trevelyan's had only just got up. Eva had explained to Steve that the website of the jewellery shop showed a short film explaining how they make the charms for these particular bracelets.

'You're disturbing our breakfast,' the husband complained. 'What do you want from me now?

'It's not you we've come to see,' Eva said, friendly but firmly.

'Can we have a word with your wife please?'

'I'm here, what can I do for you?'

'Mrs Trevelyan, I am arresting you for the murder of William Gunn.' Before she could continue she was interrupted by Mr Trevelyan.

'This is preposterous. You'll not hear the last of this,' he shouted.

'Sssh Jonathan,' said his wife, 'I knew it would come out one day.' She looked almost relieved.

'I never meant to kill him,' Mrs Trevelyan explained to the detectives after they arrived back at the station.

'I just wanted him to leave my daughter alone. Anne had such a bright future. She was marrying into a really good family. She would have gone up in the world and never wanted for anything. In the end she threw it all away anyway.'

She started crying.

'What a waste.'

Eva was not sure if she was referring to Anne's divorce or Mr Gunn's death. She hoped it was the latter.

'Can we just go back to the beginning Mrs Trevelyan. You told me that you met Mr Gunn by chance at the railway station in Downham Market?'

'Yes, I had been to my jewellery making class but had left my car in the station car park. I noticed him unlocking his bike and went over to talk to him. My husband and I were aware that he had befriended our daughter although we never told her this. I was going to offer him money to stay away from Anne but he would have none of it. He then started threatening me, saying he would tell Anne what I said. He said he loved her and that he would not have a stupid old bitch stand in his way. When he said that I couldn't take it anymore. We are a respectable family and I felt he was insulting everything we stood for.'

'So what happened?'

'I just wanted him to shut up. I had my bag of tools with me and grabbed my pattern hammer.'

She paused. 'Is that how you found out it was me?'

'Yes,' Eva replied. 'Your hammer left the same imprint on Mr Gunn's skull as the one on Anne's bracelet charms which we know you made.'

Steve had remained quiet throughout the interview. When Mrs Trevelyan was eventually led away he congratulated Eva.

'Well done! That was real detective work.'

'Thank you,' she said, trying to hide how pleased she was.

Four weeks later

Anne had agreed to meet Steve at a café in Ely. After a coffee they decided to go for a walk along the riverbank.

'I don't know what to say,' she said. 'I am so embarrassed and hurt. Imagine, my mother, a murderer.'

'She will probably be tried for manslaughter,' suggested Steve. 'A good barrister will argue that she was acting in self-defence. I wouldn't be surprised if she gets away with a very light sentence, especially considering her age.'

'I don't know what to hope for,' Anne replied. 'I hate her for what she did but at the same time, she is my mother. And I feel so sorry for my dad.'
She started crying.

'What are you going to do now?' asked Steve.

'I'm not sure yet but I'm thinking about moving in with my dad so I can keep an eye on him. Paul has been offered a place on a graduate training scheme in Milton Keynes so he will be moving there.'

'I hear the DNA test confirmed that Billy was Paul's dad. How has he taken it?'

'Much better than I expected. He told me that although he respected Geoffrey he was never able to get close to him. Milton Keynes is not that far from Peterborough so I hope to see a lot of him. But I've got to get away from here. I feel everyone is looking at me.'

They probably are, Steve thought but didn't say so. He took her hand.

'I know it must be very painful for you but I want to thank you for speaking to me that night. Without it we would never have been able to find out what actually happened.' They had arrived back at the café.

'Maybe we'll meet in another twenty-five years,' Anne said.

'Maybe we will,' he replied.

While Steve was talking to Anne, Eva was on her way to Bedford. She had already phoned Mr and Mrs Gunn to explain some of what had happened. But what was left to explain she wanted to do face to face. They met in the same room as before.

'Thank you for coming,' Mr Gunn said, 'at least we now know what happened and that the killer will be punished.'

'There is something else I want to tell you,' said Eva. They looked surprised.

'I know you didn't agree with your son's activism,' she started, 'but you might feel better to learn that it was his evidence that stopped the dumping of nuclear waste in the wrong location. We all owe him a great deal of thanks for that.'

Mr Gunn was visibly moved.

'Thank you for telling us that. I wished I could tell him myself how proud and sorry I am.'

'That's not all,' Eva continued. 'Thanks to the DNA you supplied we were able to identify William as the victim. But it also established that he is in fact the father of Anne Trevelyan's son.'

Mrs Gunn started crying.

'Does that mean…?'

'Yes it does, you have a grandson.'

She produced a photo.

'He looks exactly like our William,' Mr Gunn said.

'I have spoken to him at length,' Eva explained. 'He would very much like to meet you both. He wants to find out as much as he can about his father's family.' She looked at the elderly couple who were both in floods of tears.

'Tell him,' Mrs Gunn said finally, 'tell him, he's always welcome here.'